MW00935184

Jordan,
I hope yo
this one as m
and listen to
parents. They
know what's best!
#Trust me!.

Robert
10/3/19

Robert Starnes

An Exciting and Adventurous way to view History

Book Two of the

Saving History Series

School

Bound

Robert Starnes

Robert Starnes

Published by Starnes Books LLC
Edited by Carpenter Editing Services, LLC

ISBN: 978-1-7325803-4-3 (sc)
ISBN: 978-1-7325803-5-0 (e)

Library of Congress Control Number: 2018915327

Printed in the United States of America
First Printing 2019

Dedication

I want to take a moment to dedicate this installment of the *Saving History Series, School Bound*, to all the children, teenagers, young adults and even adults that are currently being bullied, or who have survived being bullied. I am a product of being bullied myself, so I want you to know that there is hope for you. You can survive and become someone you never knew you wanted to be, just like I did. You are never alone with what you are going through, and know that there is help out there. You have to have the strength to reach out to someone for help. If the people you are telling about the abuse are not helping you, then tell someone else. And if they do not help, then keep telling others. Never stop telling your story, even after it is heard.

As you will see, my characters know a thing or two about being different, and you will see how they cope with it. Each person is different, and we all hurt in some ways the same. Suicide is NEVER the answer. You will survive and get through these times, so NEVER give up on yourself. When you learn to love and accept everything about you that makes you so unique, you will be stronger, so when others talk about you, they will have less power over you. You are perfect in every way! Remember, when someone is saying things about someone else because they are different, the same can be said in reverse about them being different too.

We, the bullied, are just too modest to overpower others by pointing out just how much our differences are from another person. It's called "respect and acceptance." We rise above the bullies and give them the "respect" everyone deserves. We give them the "acceptance" in which all people should be, as who they are with their differences.

Contents

Robert Starnes

Prologue: Council's Choice

With the Council being unable to use Alexis to repair the change in history, since she is the one who caused the change in history by going back and erasing herself from it, their choices for help are limited. There are only a couple of other special groups they watch over that may be able to help them go back in time. The Council isn't in agreement on who they can turn to for help. They know no one can fully be trusted, when before they all could agree on Alexis for help.

Knowing the struggles they are faced with after months of debating among themselves, the Council reached a decision on who they would reach out to for help. They have agreed to seek help from three groups they have been watching for many years that have the most potential of being able to complete such a task that they will be asking them to do. Picking the groups to ask to help them go back in time to stop Alexis is just the first obstacle they are going to face. They still have a few more obstacles to overcome if they are going to succeed.

Unaware of Alexis' true intentions on why she went back in time and erased herself from history, or at least a version they are aware of that she does exist in, they can only make assumptions between themselves. The Council does not believe in assuming anything, only in facts, so this has them at a loss and confused. This is new for them, to not be in the know, or even in control.

The one thing they can agree on is going back to stop Alexis from erasing herself is their top priority at this moment, so they send out their request to the leaders of the three groups they have chosen for help. They do understand that each one will want something in return, even if they are unable to achieve their goal sending them back in time, but they have to try.

While their formal, yet urgent, request to the group leaders they chose have been sent out to attend a Special Council Meeting, they can only wait and see if they accept the invitation.

So their wait begins...

Chapter 1

Why Michael?

Ian has been awake for two hours before his mother knocked on his bedroom door. He knew today was coming quickly, and he has been anxious to go to school, so he could begin his search for Kayla. Ian knows she is still out there, somewhere in time, since it has only been a week since her last contact with him. Her last words to him where "Don't forget me, Ian," and he has no intention of doing so. He was up and ready to go to his new school with Jax.

"It's time to get up."

"Thanks, mom," Ian replies, knowing it will be some time before he is able to come back home to see his parents. Today, Jax is going to be taking him to his new school.

"What do you want for breakfast this morning?" his mother asks.

"How about my favorite, eggs over medium, toast, and today, make it a tall stack of buttermilk pancakes," Ian replies. Ian is not sure for how long it is going to take them to get to his new school, so he wants to make sure he eats enough this morning to last until, who knows when, they will stop to eat again.

Jax has told Ian very little about where the school is actually located. Ian was just told to pack for at least a full semester. Packing for long term only let Ian know he was going to be at school awhile, but not exactly how long it was going to take them to get there, not to mention how they were going to get there.

Surely, we will be flying to the school, Ian secretly hopes. *What if the school is not even in the United States? I don't even have a passport!*

Okay, calm down and relax, he tells himself. *If I needed a passport, I'm sure Jax would have told my mother and me beforehand.*

I better get a move on, Jax could be over at any moment and I still need to get ready, Ian begins to motivate himself.

Being the snappy dresser Ian is, and since today is a special day, he wants to make sure he looks his best when they arrive at his new school. *You can only make a first impression once,* Ian thinks to himself.

Before Ian's shower, he had already laid out a pair of dark jeans, a crimson long sleeve button down dress shirt, black leather dress belt, black vest and bowtie, all topped off with a pair of black socks and black tennis shoes. He wants to not only look good walking around today, but he also wants his feet to feel good.

After Ian finishes his shower and dries off, he brushes his teeth and combs his hair. Ian has shoulder length, naturally curly black hair. Being that his hair is naturally curly, Ian normally just lets it hang down, but since today will be spent traveling, he pulls it back with a rubber band. Pulling his hair back is the best way for it to stay out of his face for the long trip.

Ian takes his time getting dressed this morning, because he is a little scared to be leaving home. This will be the first time he has ever been away from home without his parents or his best friend Kayla, even though no one remembers her except him. Just as Ian is about to put on his ring, there is a knock on his bedroom door. Ian sets the ring down next to the Time Keeper on the dresser.

The Time Keeper is the watch that was created by Peter Hele, Ian's distant relative. Ian has recently found out the watch's history and how his family bloodline can access it. Not only can he access the Time Keeper, but the memories that have been stored in it by his past relatives, who had possession and control of it during their time period. His ancestors have had the ability to gain access to the Time Keeper where they could store any memory they wanted to store in it and access their own memories as well. Not many of his ancestors ever used the Time Keeper to go back into their memories to change the outcome for fear of the effects it could have in their current time. Really, only one of Ian's ancestors used it enough for the Council to take notice of the Time Keepers' existence, and that was Sebastian Helen. Of course, Sebastian never used it in a way to change history, except only to keep his friendship intact with Greyson Zimmerman. It works up until one night's fight causes Sebastian to lose the Time Keeper, not forever, but for a very long time.

Up until recently, it has always been believed that one could only access their own memories that they stored in the Time Keeper. That all changed when Ian lost a year of his life, after leaving his apartment to look for his parents, on his first seventeenth birthday, only to come home to his surprise eighteenth birthday party. Confusing as it was already, when Ian went to bed that night, he woke up back on his seventeenth birthday again, not being able to remember any of year he lost from turning seventeen to eighteen.

Now the ring, which Ian sets the Time Keeper next to on the dresser, is the birthday gift Kayla gives him on his eighteenth birthday, next year. That silver ring, when placed on Ian's hand while he is wearing the Time Keeper, wiped Kayla from history and sent him back to his seventeenth birthday. Kayla was able to contact Ian and explain some of why she did what she did. She also explained that now Ian has an extra year to go back to the school to learn more about what's to come, so he'll know more than he knew the first time. This is the time he lost between seventeen and eighteen.

He has been ready to get to school since Kayla last contacted him, in his dream, a week ago.

The knocking continues as Ian asks, "Who is it?"

"It's me, Michael," is the reply.

Michael? What in the world could he be doing here? Ian wonders in confusion. He turns to open his bedroom door, almost tripping over the bag he has already packed for school.

"What are you doing here?" Ian questions Michael.

Michael has been Ian's biggest bully throughout school. Ian had never done anything to him, but Michael had it out for him for as long as Ian can remember. *This must have something to do with the change in history. At least I hope it does,* Ian contemplates.

"Well, do you really think I'm going to let you leave for a new school and not come by and see you off?" Michael answers. "Besides, we never got to finish our talk about what happened to you the other day, remember, on your birthday?"

"Yes, I remember, but there really isn't much to talk about," Ian is holding back the truth from Michael, because he has no clue what he is talking about. "After you left and I went to talk to my parents, they surprised me with this whole 'new school' thing."

"All right then, if you say so, Ian. So, tell me about this private school where your parents are sending you," Michael says with excitement for Ian.

Ian knows very little about the school he is about to go to or even where it's located. He never asked Jax about it. Once time was thought to be healed, from the intentional history wipe, the question never came up.

"You know Math, English, History, the usual classes like any other school. Just new people," Ian tells him.

"Enough about me and the school, let's talk about you," Ian playfully suggests to Michael. "What are you going to do?"

"Well, for starters, I just may start getting to school on time, now that I won't have to wait for you to get ready in the mornings," Michael smirks at Ian.

"To be perfectly honest, Ian, I haven't really thought about it. I mean, it's going to take some getting used to, you not being here. I guess I will just have to hang out with my other friends more," Michael admits.

"Breakfast is ready," Ian's mother is yelling from the kitchen before Ian can make any remarks back to Michael.

"Do you want to stay for breakfast? We are having my favorite!" Ian asks Michael, trying to persuade him into believing he knows they are friends.

"I can't, sorry. My mom is taking me shopping for some reason," Michael tells Ian. "Will I see you on winter break?" Michael asks Ian with a sad look on his face.

"I'm not sure, but let's just say that when I do come back, you will be the first person I call. I promise," Ian says to Michael.

"Deal, now go eat your breakfast before it gets cold. I'm headed into the city with my mother for the day. Wish me luck," Michael orders Ian.

As they both say their goodbyes and give each other a farewell hug, Ian couldn't help but wonder what else has changed, now that Kayla is no longer in his past or in history for that matter. Now that Michael is his best friend, Ian misses Kayla even more.

As Ian takes a seat at the table to enjoy his breakfast, he hears the front door close behind Michael as he leaves.

Just as Ian is about to take a big bite of his pancakes, Jax comes rushing in the front door. "Ian, are you all right?"

"Yes, why does everyone keep asking me that?" Ian replies. "What's wrong?"

"I'm not sure, yet. There has been a change in time. Did you go back and change something?"

"No, I couldn't even if I wanted to, remember I'm only seventeen. I won't be able to access the Time Keeper until I'm eighteen," Ian answers, while running to his room to grab the watch. "Anyway, you can see for yourself the Time Keeper is right here, and so is the ring!" Ian yells while holding the watch out in front of him in one hand and the ring in the other for Jax to see. After seeing them, Jax is satisfied knowing Ian still had them and had not used them. Ian wraps the watch around his wrist and slips the ring over his right hand ring finger first knuckle.

How am I going to explain this to Michael that my new History teacher came bursting in my front door, just as he was leaving? Ian wonders to himself.

"What did you say to Michael when you passed him as you were coming in just now?" Ian asks Jax.

"I didn't pass anyone on my way in," Jax answers looking puzzled at Ian.

"That's not possible! He just walked out of the apartment when you burst in! You had to have passed him, if not in the hall, then in the stairwell. He has to live somewhere near here!"

"Are you sure, Ian? Who is Michael anyway?" Jax asks Ian sharply.

"Yes, I'm sure. He just left. For some reason, since Kayla is no longer part of my history, I think this guy Michael from school is now my best friend, except, I don't remember anything about us being friends," Ian explains to Jax. "It's a long story."

"What is all the commotion about? Jax, what's happening?" Ian's mother demands to know as she is flying out of the kitchen.

"Mom, is Michael in the kitchen with you? Did he come back inside?" Ian needs to know.

"No. It's just me in here. I haven't seen Michael this morning. Was he here?" she inquires.

"What do you mean you haven't seen him this morning? Didn't you let him in about twenty minutes ago?" Ian asks.

"What are you talking about, Ian? No one has been here that I know."

"Michael was just here, in my room. He said he came over to see me before I left for school. If you didn't let him in, then who did?"

"Why in the world would Michael, of all people, come over here to see you off to school? You two have never been friends," his mother replies back with a little concern in her voice.

This is the moment when Ian begins to think of a new conclusion.

Ian grabs Jax by the arm and pulls him over to the hall, towards his room. Jax gives him a look of surprise, but follows along with his guidance.

Once they are alone, and out of earshot of his mother, Ian decides to tell Jax what he believes to be happening. "You told me that time had healed and had caught up to our new reality, the one without Kayla, correct?" Ian asks Jax.

"Yes, I told you that yesterday, which is what the Council told me. Why do you ask?"

"I don't think that was the truth. I think time is just now catching up to our reality and healing, because that is the only explanation as to why you did not run into Michael just now as you were entering the apartment. Michael had just left here and closed the door, and then a few seconds later you came in, but you didn't see him at all. If you didn't see him, then where did he go? While we are on the subject, do you remember where you were just before you came through our door?" Ian questions Jax.

"Of course I remember where I was. I was coming over here. I was…"

"Was what?" Ian asks for Jax to continue.

"Well, I know I was headed here, because I had just received a call from the Council about another force felt by them. The only thing is that

I don't remember the trip here. I do remember reaching for my front door, to leave my apartment, then being here," Jax explains.

"And that doesn't sound or feel odd to you?"

"Not really. When I think about it, the memory of me coming here is in my mind, except it is more of a fast memory. It is like watching a movie, but in fast forward. It's hard to explain, but I do and don't remember coming over here. It is just when I think about it, it's in fast forward and I can't control it, so I can't stop it at any point, or even slow it down. Do you understand?"

"Well, kind of. It sounds a lot like what I went through with the memory wipe, except instead of your memories going in reverse, yours were going forward, fast forward," Ian reiterates to Jax.

"If what you are suggesting is true, and time is just now catching up and actually healing, then we may already be behind schedule," Jax relays to Ian.

Right then, Jax decides it is time for them to leave and head for the school. Jax hopes Ian's mother still knows about Ian going off to school.

"Well, we really should be hitting the road. We have a long trip ahead of us today. What do you say, Ian, are you ready to go?" Jax shoots Ian a look of, please trust me.

"Okay, let me grab my bag," replies Ian, as he runs back to his room to get his packed bag.

Now that Ian has everything and they are heading out of the apartment, they run into Michael, Ian's now best friend, as he was walking up to the door.

"Ian, where are you going? You weren't going to run off to school without telling me bye, were you?" Michael has a shocked look in his eyes as he questions Ian.

Feeling overwhelmed, Ian suddenly feels dizzy. Panic is starting to take over his mind, and that is when IT happened. Ian didn't know what was going on. One minute he's running out of the apartment with Jax, and the next minute everyone freezes, except for Ian.

What did I do this time? Ian wonders, in amazement, to himself.

"What did 'you' do?" replies a voice Ian has never heard before. "You mean 'what did I do,'" says the voice again. The voice sounds like it is coming from the stairwell.

About that time, a young girl comes walking out from the stairwell door. The young girl couldn't be more than ten years old. The girl is small, but has the biggest hazel green eyes and long curly blonde hair. She looks lost and anxious, her big hazel eyes looking everywhere around her, while biting her nails. She is trying to remain calm.

"What's your name?" Ian asks the little young blonde girl.

"Kenzie," replies the girl. "My name is Kenzie."

Chapter 2

Who are You?

"It's nice to meet you, Kenzie. My name is..."

But before Ian could finish his sentence, she finishes it for him. "Ian," Kenzie says.

How does she know my name? Ian wonders.

"I don't really know how I know. It just popped into my head, so I guessed that was your name," replies Kenzie. "Am I right? Is that your name?"

"It is," Ian replies.

"I know," Kenzie smirks back.

"Okay, well how is it that you are here reading my thoughts, and how and why is everyone frozen?" Ian anxiously wants to get to the bottom of this.

"I don't know the answers to those questions either. What I can remember is, one minute I'm at home with my little brother, Connor, and then, the next thing I know I am on those stairs, scared." As Kenzie spoke, she was pointing at the entrance to the stairwell. "When I heard you coming out into the hallway, not knowing where I was, I didn't know what to do. I thought to myself that if I had a few more minutes, maybe I could get back home. The next thing I knew all I could hear was silence, and then I heard you ask, 'What did I do,' to yourself, so I answered you. The rest you already know because it just happened," Kenzie says with an exhausting look on her face.

"I wouldn't say I know the rest, not exactly. For the record, I did not ask myself what I did out loud, I was thinking it to myself." Ian felt the need to clarify the difference to Kenzie. "So, do you know how long they are going to be frozen, or is this all new to you also?" Ian hopes she has some answers about her powers.

"If I remember correctly, I believe I did this to my brother once, by accident. We were playing in our treehouse, and I inadvertently stepped on one of his toys. To get even with me, Connor was going to throw one of my dolls out of our treehouse, but then he became frozen. At the time, all I wanted was to get my doll away from him before he threw her out of the window. Next thing you know, he wasn't moving. Don't worry though. It didn't last long, about thirty minutes, maybe?" Kenzie answers with uncertainty.

"How far does your freeze ability go? I mean, like, is the world frozen, or is it just us?" Ian is hoping for the latter.

"I'm pretty sure it's just us. When I froze Connor, I heard my mom and dad come out of the house and into the back yard looking for us," she replies looking pleased.

"Okay, but until we know for sure when they are going to unfreeze, we need to get Jax and Michael into the apartment. We need to make sure they are not out here in case any of my neighbors come out into the hall and see them and start freaking out," Ian insists to Kenzie.

With an accepting nod, Kenzie walks over closer to Ian, Jax, and Michael. She is not sure how much help she can be, since they are all so much bigger than she is, but she is going to try her best to help Ian. She feels bad that she got Ian into this mess. The least she can do is try and help him in any way she can.

First, Ian walks up to Michael and tips him over onto his side, and then lays him gently on the ground. In his frozen state, he seems much lighter than he normally is, which is great for Kenzie. Since he is so light, she can actually help Ian get him into the apartment. Kenzie walks over and grabs Michael by his feet, while Ian is holding him by his shoulders. Together they carry Michael into the apartment, standing him next to Ian's frozen mother. Now they need to move Jax inside before anyone sees them.

Ian thinks since Michael is so light, he can assume they can carry Jax just as easily. Knowing what they say about making assumptions, Ian was reminded quickly how true it is. When they start to tip Jax over, he is light enough that he floats to the ceiling. As Jax is rising past the point of Kenzie's reach, Ian jumps up, throws his body over Jax and pulls him back down, while pushing him through the apartment door all at the same time.

Now that Jax and Michael are out of the hall, Ian and Kenzie have to think fast about how to anchor Jax down. With one foot holding Jax to the floor, Ian swiftly reaches over and picks Kenzie up, placing her on Jax's chest as an anchor. "That should hold him down for a minute while I figure out another way to keep him off the ceiling. Don't move, okay, Kenzie?" Ian asks playfully, while trying to make her laugh.

"Okay, but what are you going to do?" Kenzie has a feeling that her tiny body will not hold Jax down for long.

"I'm going to run to my room and grab some things we can use to tie Jax down. I'll be right back," Ian boasts, already running down the hall to his room.

Once Ian makes it to his room, he pushes open the door and heads straight for his closet. As he opens his closet door, he reaches in and grabs the first things he can get ahold of, turns and runs back out of his room, down the hall, and back to the living room. As Ian enters the room, Jax, still frozen with Kenzie sitting on top of him, has begun to float about two feet off the floor. Kenzie looks as if she is having the time of her life. She is not scared in the least.

"I hate to interrupt your fun time, but can you tie a knot?" Ian asks Kenzie.

"Yes, I can tie a knot. I'm not a baby, you know. I can even tie my own shoes! Want me to show you?" Kenzie snaps back to Ian in a matter-of-fact tone.

"No, that's okay. I believe you. Now, when I get Jax back on the floor, I am going to need you to hop off and start tying these things together," Ian orders Kenzie as he is pointing at a pile of garments he has gathered from his room that are now on the living room floor.

Kenzie looks over to the garments and finds a bit of humor in his choice. "Ties? You want me to tie ties together?" Kenzie sounds amused.

"Yes, ties," Ian shoots back at Kenzie. "Okay? Ready? Set? Hop off."

While Ian is holding Jax down with his foot, Kenzie heads over to the pile of ties that Ian has brought back from his room and has thrown on the floor and starts to tie them together.

Ian instructs Kenzie to make four groups of ties, all the same length.

Kenzie grabs tie after tie and knots them together at their ends, tugs on them to make sure they are strong enough to hold, then ties another. She continues this process until she has completed the task Ian gave her. "All done," Kenzie shouts over to Ian.

"Okay, now I am going to float Jax over to you, and I will need you to tie one group of ties around each of his wrists and ankles. Think you can do that for me while I hold Jax in place?" Ian asks.

"Sure, but can you get him over here without letting him hit the ceiling? Better yet, can you get him over here without letting him float out of the window?" Kenzie jokes back at Ian.

"Very funny! Just tie those things around him please," Ian is losing patience with Kenzie's wit.

As Kenzie finishes tying the last group of ties around Jax's left ankle, Ian is already positioning Jax over the couch. "Okay, now help me tie each one of these," Ian tells Kenzie, while holding one of the tie groups, "to the legs of the couch. This way, at least when he unfreezes, he will land on the couch instead of hitting the floor."

"Good idea, Ian!" Kenzie exclaims with excitement.

As they finish anchoring Jax down with the ties to the couch, and Ian is satisfied Jax will not float away or out of the window, he is ready to find out more about his new friend.

Ian and Kenzie each take a seat at the dining room table. Neither of them look directly at each other at first, but they can tell they each look exhausted and full of questions.

"Now that that is all taken care of, for now anyway, what do you say about us talking and getting to know each other a bit?" Ian is ready to learn more about Kenzie.

"Okay, that sounds like a plan. What do you want to know?"

"Let's start with, where do you live? You said you remember being with your little brother, Connor, before being here," Ian gives Kenzie a place to start.

"Sure, but first, where is here?" Kenzie wants to know where she is after teleporting.

"Well, we are in Brooklyn. Do you know where Brooklyn is?" Ian asks. Not knowing what grade Kenzie is in, he is not sure if she even knows all of the States yet.

"No, is it close to Dallas?" Kenzie answers back.

"Not exactly. Is Dallas where you live?" asks Ian.

"No, but my cousins live there. I live in Enloe. It's a small town in Texas, just outside of Cooper, but it's close to Dallas. Do you know where Dallas is?"

"Yes, I do know where Dallas is, and let's just say it is not very close to here. Let me start by telling you a bit about myself. I am a junior in high school," Ian explains to Kenzie. "I have lived here my entire life with my mom and dad, and up until recently, my best friend Kayla. Don't even ask about that situation right now. I'm sure your family is worried sick about you. Do you know your phone number?" Ian wants to let her parents know that Kenzie is safe so they can relax, if they have even noticed that she is missing.

"Yes, but before we call them, what am I going to tell them? I was there at home with Connor one minute, and now I am here with you, and them," Kenzie says while pointing at the frozen people in the room. "How is that going to sound to my parents?"

"Good question. I say we wait until Jax is unfrozen. Maybe he can help us out with that," Ian sounds uneasy about having to wait to call Kenzie's parents, but he knows it is the right thing to do.

"So, where do you go to school, and what grade are you in?" Ian asks Kenzie.

"I go to Cooper Elementary, and I am in the fifth grade. We are the Fighting Bull Dawgs," Kenzie replies with some school spirit. "And yes I said DAWGS, because that's how we pronounce it, dawgs."

"Okay, so you go to Cooper (coup-er)," as Ian pronounces her school, "and you are in the fifth grade. Is it a big school?" Ian asks.

"First of all, it's pronounced *COOPER*, you know, like *book, look, cook*, not *couk, louk, bouk*," Kenzie corrects Ian quickly. "And no, I don't think it's a big school. There are about twenty-five kids in my class."

"Okay, thank you for the correction and the lesson on how to say your school's name. So, um, let's switch gears now. Were you born with these freezing powers?" Ian asks Kenzie, feeling jealous since his abilities come from a watch.

"I don't think so. I mean, last year my mom gave me this necklace for my birthday. She told me some story about it, but I can't remember it now. I do remember this only happening after I put on the necklace. Do you think the necklace has something to do with it?" Kenzie is hoping Ian knows the answer. "Do you have any powers?"

"Well, somehow, with this watch, I am able to go back in time. I have only done it once, by mistake, kind of like when you froze Connor, your little brother. Jax knows about the Time Keeper, that's what he calls the watch, and me having it. My parents asked Jax to come and take me to a private school for special kids. Jax is the History teacher there. My mom was supposed to give me this watch next year for my eighteenth birthday, and she did. But that's when things became strange for me, and I am now having my seventeenth birthday over again. Things get a little confusing when you go back in time and change it. From what we can gather, I did not go back and change anything. I was tricked into putting on this ring and that caused me to have my history wiped of the past year. So here we are," Ian is finishing up just as Jax falls down on the couch with a thump.

"Why am I tied to the couch, and how did I get here anyway?" Jax asks looking directly at Ian.

Both Kenzie and Ian burst out laughing. *Guess it's time for Jax to be filled in,* Ian thinks to himself.

"I guess so," replies Kenzie out loud.

Robert Starnes

Chapter 3

What Happened?

Ian filled Jax in on his new friend Kenzie and what had happened to him, Ian's mother, and Michael. Meanwhile, Kenzie was getting something to eat in the kitchen with Ian's mother. Michael is the only one who has not returned to normal, as he remains frozen. Teleporting must take a lot out of Kenzie, because she has Ian's mom making all kinds of sandwiches and has chosen several different types of chips to go along with the sandwiches.

Once Kenzie has her meal ready, she wastes no time in starting to eat it.

"Would you like to go have a seat at the table in the dining room to finish eating?" Ian's mother asks Kenzie.

"No thank you. I am fine eating right here at the kitchen counter. If that is okay with you."

Ian's mother gives Kenzie a smile of approval. That is all she needs to continue scarfing down her food. She continues to eat non-stop until her plate is completely empty.

Just as Ian is finishing explaining things to Jax, Kenzie comes bouncing out of the kitchen and into the living room. Kenzie seems to be in high spirits after eating, regardless of all the recent events that have been happening. Kenzie takes a seat next to Ian on the couch, while Jax is sitting attentively on the chair right beside them.

Jax doesn't seem too surprised about the news of the events that have just taken place. You could have thought, by the look on Jax's face, that this may not have been the first time he has been frozen.

Jax insists that he contact Kenzie's parents to explain things. Ian and Kenzie both agree with Jax's decision. Jax gets up from the chair and proceeds over to the phone. Once he reaches the table the phone is sitting on, Kenzie gives Jax her parents' phone number. As Jax explains things to Kenzie's parents, Ian and Kenzie take this time to get to know each other more.

"Do you think my parents know about any of this stuff?" Kenzie asks Ian.

"It's possible. I mean, after all, my parents know about the Time Keeper," Ian replies to Kenzie, which seems to make her feel a little bit more at ease.

"I hope they are not mad at me for leaving like that," Kenzie says softly to Ian. "They have not been in the best of moods lately for some reason. It's like, no matter what Connor or I do, they just are not happy with either one of us, or anything else for that matter."

"I'm sure they're not mad at you, Kenzie. It's not like you just ran away from home on purpose, or did you?" Ian playfully asks Kenzie. "It's not like you knew that was going to even happen. I'm sure everything will be fine once Jax explains to them that you are safe here with us," Ian reassures Kenzie.

"While we let Jax handle your parents, tell me more about how it is that you can hear my thoughts," Ian inquires of Kenzie. "Is that part of the power of your necklace?"

"Oh, that is something I have always been able to do. It's hard to control sometimes. One minute I can only hear my own thoughts, then BAM, next thing you know I'm listening to someone else's thoughts. I thought I was going crazy the first time it happened. It only lasted for a minute, but it was the longest minute in my dad's head than I would have ever wanted to have happen," Kenzie tells Ian jokingly.

"Now that's funny!" Ian exclaims.

"Sure, *you* think it's funny. But try listening to your dad's thoughts on bills, work, mom, and a man named Mason," Kenzie replies to Ian. "It's not funny at all!"

"Now that you put it that way, maybe it's not really funny. But I thought I was going crazy too when you first started answering the questions I was thinking."

"Sorry about that, Ian. It's like I said. It's hard to control sometimes," Kenzie apologizes to Ian.

"It's okay. Now you mentioned that your dad was thinking of a man named Mason," Ian inquires. "Do you know why he was thinking about this man?"

"No, like I said, I did not want to be in his mind at all much less listen to any of his thoughts. Remember, my mom was in those thoughts too," Kenzie clears things up quickly.

"This is very important, Kenzie. I'm sorry, but I need you to try and remember what your dad was thinking at the time Mason's name came up," Ian pushes Kenzie for a little more information.

"I really don't think I can. I was younger, and it was the first time that I had ever heard anyone else's thoughts before," Kenzie explains to Ian. "But I will try for you. Let me think."

"Thank you."

Kenzie closes her eyes so she can concentrate. She is beginning to remember bits and pieces of that moment. She can see herself at home sitting on the living room floor playing a game of some sort while her dad is sitting on the sofa talking on the phone. It is then, just as he hangs up the phone, that she first finds herself in her dad's mind.

"Okay, I remember something. My dad was talking on the phone. I don't know who he was talking to, but as soon as he hung up the phone, I could begin to hear his thoughts," Kenzie reveals to Ian.

"That's good Kenzie. Now, what are you hearing inside of your father's mind?"

"Give me a minute. I said I'm just remembering when I first heard his thoughts, not his actual thoughts yet," Kenzie snaps back at Ian while keeping her eyes closed.

Kenzie is back in her thoughts, back in their living room at home, but she feels strange inside. She is realizing the reason she feels this way is because she is hearing her dad thinking to himself. Fear is beginning to fill her emotionally as she is looking around the room trying to figure out what is happening. Since Kenzie knows these are just memories, she takes control over the fear in her younger self. She starts to focus on the thoughts she is hearing. At first they are all muddled and jumbled together. There are thoughts of her mom, bills and work all in her dad's mind, just how she remembered. But now when the thought of Mason comes around, she senses fear in her dad.

"FEAR!"

"What do you mean?" Ian inquires.

Kenzie opens her eyes and turns her attention to Ian. "Fear was what my father was feeling when he thought of Mason," Kenzie reiterates to Ian. "That is all I can remember. My dad felt fear when he thought of Mason."

"Okay, Kenzie, thank you for remembering. Are you going to be okay?"

"Yes, I'm going to be fine, but can we please talk about something else?" Kenzie pleads.

"Yes, of course we can. Let's talk about how I was starting to think I was talking out loud and didn't realize it when you first answered my thoughts. I feel much better now knowing you were just in my head, and I am not going crazy," Ian comforts Kenzie.

Ian and Kenzie continue with their small talk until Jax comes back from calling Kenzie's parents. Jax was on the phone for over thirty minutes. This gave Ian and Kenzie enough time to get to know more about each other, things they did not have not a chance to discuss earlier, and begin to feel like friends.

"So, Jax, how did Kenzie's parents react to the news about Kenzie being in Brooklyn? Do they seem surprised?" Ian is firing questions at Jax.

"Well, I didn't actually tell them that she is in Brooklyn with us. I don't want to tell them more than they need to know for now. I will feel more comfortable about Kenzie's parents once I speak to the Council about them. It seems odd that no one from the school has ever been contacted about Kenzie and her powers," Jax says to the pair of them.

"Kenzie, do your parents know about any of your powers? Have you ever talked to them before about what you can do?" Jax inquires.

"Not that I can remember. I mean, I've never used them in front of them, and they have never asked. When my mom gave me this necklace, she told me some story about it, but I don't remember any of the story now. I can say that I only began to freeze time after she gave the necklace to me," Kenzie answers Jax.

"If you didn't tell them she is here, where do they think she is?" Ian questions Jax.

"I told them she is safe and close by. I also said she would be home shortly," Jax explains.

"Okay. So now what do we do?" Kenzie asks Ian.

"What do you think, Jax?" Ian is hoping Jax has all the answers.

Before Jax can answer Ian's question, Michael suddenly wakes up from being frozen.

"What is going on here? How did I get inside, and how did all you guys get on the couch so fast?" Michael is freaking out, just a little.

Before Ian can turn his attention to Michael to answer his questions, Michael is frozen once again. So are Jax and Ian's mother!

"Kenzie, why did you freeze them again?" Ian shouts at Kenzie, "Kenzie? Kenzie!" But she is gone.

"Why are you shouting, Ian?" questions Ian's mother. "Where did your little friend, Kenzie, go?"

"I don't know. Jax, do you know what happened to Kenzie?" Ian is now worried about Kenzie.

"What is going on around here?" Michael asks to anyone who will listen, as he is unfrozen again for the second time. "Who was that girl, and how did she disappear like that?" This time it is Michael asking the questions.

"Michael! You need to leave now. I will explain everything to you later, but right now you need to go home," Ian tells Michael, while ushering him out the door.

"Why can't you tell me now?" Michael wants some answers.

"Michael, we don't have time for this. Please, just go home," Ian insists. "I'll call you later, but for now, bye," Ian tells Michael as he is showing him out and shutting the door on him.

"Ian, that was very rude. Why did you do that to Michael?" Ian's mother demands to know.

"Mom, Michael is not my best friend. Kayla is my best friend, and she's missing, along with Kenzie. It's a Time Keeper problem, understand?" Ian scolds his mother.

Even though she does not like Ian talking to her like that, she knows there are some things she will never understand. She knows Ian is meant for great things, but being rude will not be one of them. "We will talk about this later, Ian. Do you understand?" Ian's mother ends the conversation as she walks out of the room.

Ian feels bad speaking to his mother like that. He will apologize to her later, but right now he needs to focus on Kayla and Kenzie. *Where could they be?* Ian wonders to himself. He is secretly wanting Kenzie to answer back, but she doesn't.

Chapter 4

Ready to Go?

"Ian, are you all right?" Jax asks since Ian has such a puzzled look on his face. "Don't worry about Kenzie. I'm sure she went back home. I will give her parents a quick call to make sure, but then we have to leave. We need to get to the school so we can try and figure out how history changed when you put on that ring, which wiped a year of your life and Kayla's existence," Jax finishes as he is walking over towards the phone.

Jax is on the phone with Kenzie's parents, as Ian sits and wonders, *Why me and why now?* Ian feels some relief to find out that Kenzie is safely back at home with her parents. Ian overhears Jax confirming that fact with Kenzie's parents on the phone. *At least that's one less person I have to worry about, for now anyway.*

Ian is already standing up with his bag in his hand when Jax comes back into the living room. But before Ian can leave, he has to go apologize to his mother for being rude to her earlier. He cannot leave with her being upset with him.

Ian tells Jax to wait for him out in the hall, and he will be right out. Jax does as Ian asks, and Ian makes his way into the kitchen to look for his mother. She is standing in front of the kitchen sink cleaning up after having made sandwiches, when Ian walks up behind her. Ian gently taps her on the shoulder, hoping he does not scare her.

"Mom? I just want to say that I'm sorry for the way I snapped at you and Michael. I wasn't trying to be rude. It's just that my real best friend is gone. Gone from history. It's like she never existed. You don't even remember her now, but you did know Kayla. Jax and I are heading out now to go to the school where he teaches. We have to find out what is happening, and who went back in time to erase Kayla, and why they did it. You understand that, don't you, mom?" Ian says sadly to his mother.

"Yes, Ian. I understand. At least I think I do anyway. I'm sorry that all of this is happening to you. Your father and I should have told you sooner about the Time Keeper and its history, but we were scared. Your father had heard the stories when he was a boy. But since the Time Keeper hadn't been seen or spoken of in many years, we decided that maybe this was the time to stop telling the stories. We hoped the burden of the Time Keeper would be lifted from our family bloodline. We can see now that we thought wrong. We should have told you about your father's family history a long time ago," Ian's mother explains.

"It's okay, mom, really. It's not your fault this is happening. Everything will be fine once we can get Kayla back," Ian says trying to comfort his mother.

I was hoping that Dad would be back in time to say goodbye, but I know his new work is very important to him, Ian thinks to himself. Ian gives his mother a long, loving hug, and she hugs him back tightly. "Tell Dad I said bye, and I will be back soon," Ian tells his mother as he lets her go. They both know it is time for Ian to leave.

Ian's mother is drying her eyes as he leaves the kitchen and heads for the front door. Ian takes one last look over his shoulder at his mother, hoping she can see he will be fine. She gives Ian a quick smile and a wave good-bye. Then Ian is out the door and into the hall where Jax is waiting for him.

***

As Kenzie is coming around from the effects of teleporting, she can hear her mother on the phone. She is telling the person on the other end that Kenzie is safe. Hearing her mother speaking is the first sign that she knows she is home.

Kenzie looks around the room, just to make sure she is at home. *How am I home now?* She wonders. Even though it is only the second time she has teleported, the first time ending up in Brooklyn with Jax and Ian, she wants to know how she did it. *What did I do this time to trigger my powers?*

As Kenzie's mother is hanging up the phone, Kenzie knows her parents will start with all their questions. She also has a few of her own for them. Before Kenzie's mother turns to her, Kenzie tries to freeze time, just so she can get ready for the interrogation. But she can't. She tries again, but her mother continues walking towards her.

"You can stop trying to freeze me because you will not be able to. You still have much to learn," Kenzie's mother expresses to her.

"How do you know what I am trying to do?" Kenzie asks.

"Do you think we agreed to raise you without knowing what you were capable of doing once you were older?" replies her mother in a very aggressive tone.

"I don't understand. What do you mean agreed to raise me? Isn't that what parents are supposed to do with their children?"

"You are correct. But you are not our child. We started raising you only after our leader said your parents were not worthy of raising such a special child, but that we were," replies Kenzie's mother.

As Kenzie looks at the woman, the woman she has thought of as her real mother, in horror. She can feel anger rising inside her. As her anger rises, she thinks of Connor, her little brother. Is Connor even her real brother, or did he come from these monsters who claim to be worthy of raising her? "What about Connor? Is he even my brother, or is that another lie from you?" Kenzie demands to know.

"Why does that matter to you Kenzie? You are the only special child we are raising. Connor is simply ordinary," replies the woman pretending to be her mother. "Your father and I—"

"You are not my parents," Kenzie interrupts the woman.

"As I was saying, we were asked by our leader, many years ago, if we would raise you both as our own children, and we said yes. You see, you were given to us as a gift. Our beloved leader had asked us to complete a task for him, and you two were his way of repaying us for completing that task. Your father and I are unable to have children of our own, but we so desired to have children. Our beloved leader, Mason, knew of our heartache of not being able to have our own children, and being such a great man, he gave us both you. You may not have been our blood child, but we were grateful nonetheless," the fake mother tries to explain.

She continues, "Now as far as Connor is concerned, we were not aware of you having a bother at the time we agreed to raise you. But you were both given to us at the same time by Mason. We assumed you two were siblings. So, to be honest, we really don't know if you are or aren't siblings. We were just so blessed to be given two children to raise, we really didn't care to ask," finishes Kenzie's imposter mother.

Kenzie will need some time to process all of this. Not only process being taken from her real parents and given to these strangers, but also about Connor. Is he her brother or just another child taken from his real parents at the request of this Mason person? On top of everything, why would Mason want her taken away from her biological parents?

"Do you mind if I ask you a question?" Kenzie inquires.

"Just one? I thought for sure you would have many questions," the phony mother replies.

"Why does my power to freeze time not work on you?" Kenzie asks, hoping to find a way around that from her answer.

"Well, that's an easy one. You see we cannot freeze because we simply are not of this time. You can only freeze the time that relates to you. Since we are not from your time, you cannot freeze us. Now do you see what makes Mason such a great leader? It is that he thinks of everything. He has such amazing plans for our world. Since time is on his side, he is able to think of everything that could keep it from becoming a reality and change it," replies the out of time woman, whom she thought was her real mom.

"Well then, now that that has been explained, may I go to my room?" Kenzie asks.

"No, not until we can figure out how you got out of your room the first time. I'm going to have to ask you to go down to the basement for a little while. There are no windows for you to break through or any way for you to get out of there," replies the woman.

"Fine, I just need to get some rest. Then I will have my other questions ready for you. Maybe by then your husband will be home. I would like to hear what he has to say about all of this," Kenzie unloads on the woman as she stands up to walk towards the basement.

While Kenzie is being escorted to the basement by the woman from the wrong time, they do not speak or even share a glance at each other. Just the thought of speaking to this woman makes Kenzie sick to her stomach. All she can think about is how horrible these people are. Kenzie is ready to be away from this woman, no matter what room she had to stay in or for how long.

The woman opens the door to the basement and orders Kenzie to stay down there until the woman's husband gets home. Kenzie does as she is told. When she is about halfway down the stairs into the basement, the woman shuts the door, and Kenzie hears the lock latch.

Since Kenzie is not aware of how long she may be in the basement, she decides she can use this time to practice her other powers, the ones that her phony parents don't know about.

Maybe, just maybe, she can get ahold of Ian with her mind or maybe teleport back to him. First, she needs to figure out how she did it previously.

Kenzie tries everything she can think of to activate her powers. She tries for hours, until she is so tired, she lays down and falls asleep on the basement floor. Maybe her dreams can help her find some answers.

***

Ian still does not understand where the school is located and has no idea where they are headed, but he feels good about going with Jax. Ian and Jax take a cab to Penn Station and from there all Ian knows is they are taking a train to the school. Once they arrive at the station, Jax tips the driver and escorts Ian into the station's lobby.

As Ian enters the station, the first thing he notices is, even though the station is modern, it still has some very old clocks that fit in the arches along the ceiling. He can tell that over the years the station has been updated, but they kept a lot of the original pieces. That makes the station look amazing.

While Ian is taking in the beauty of Penn Station, he almost misses Jax handing him a train ticket. Ian snaps back to reality and looks at the ticket. Ian is ready to find out where they are going.

"Texas?" Ian shouts at Jax. "Are we going to meet up with Kenzie?"

"No. The school is in Texas. It's not in the same part of Texas where Kenzie lives, but Texas just the same. It's going to take a few days to get there, so we have a sleeper car for the trip," Jax informs Ian. "Our first stop will be in Chicago. We will have a four hour layover there to switch trains. While we are in Chicago, we will be picking up another student."

"Picking up another student? Just how many people are going on this trip?" Ian doesn't sound too pleased to have to share a sleeping car with yet another person. He feels sure that he and Jax are enough for one small room.

"Don't worry, Ian. Brayden is the only other student we are picking up along the way. He has already been attending the school for three years. He was just home visiting his parents while I went to get you," Jax answers Ian.

Jax continues, "Enough talking for now, we need to get to our platform so we don't miss our train. Once we are aboard and moving, we can talk more about Brayden and the school. Is that a deal?"

"Fine."

While Ian and Jax make their way through Penn Station to their platform, Ian cannot shake the feeling that he is being watched. Ian stops a few times to look at his surroundings, but no one stands out. Even though he cannot put his finger on it, he will not let his guard down. Ian does not feel the need to fill Jax in on his uneasy feeling, yet. *I'm sure I'm just overthinking things. With all that has been going on today, it's hard not to be on edge,* Ian thinks to himself.

"Here we go. Okay, Ian, this is our train. Let's go ahead and get aboard and find our car. We still have a few minutes before the train leaves," Jax tells Ian.

"Perfect," Ian replies. All Ian wants to do is get to their car and out of view of the public. *Better safe than sorry,* Ian thinks.

Jax and Ian step onto the train and are greeted by a conductor. Jax shows him their tickets and the conductor points down the train car and gives Jax the directions to the sleeper cars. Jax retrieves their tickets back from the conductor and heads in the direction they are told to go to their car.

Ian cannot wait to get to their private room in the sleeper car. He has been carrying his bag for some time now, and it was getting heavy. Just as Ian is ready to drop his bag, even for just a minute or two, Jax says, "Here's our room."

Pushing past Jax, Ian makes a beeline to the bottom bunk and drops his bag on it. Relief runs through Ian's arm as he lets go of his bag. Now if he could feel the same relief throughout his body as he does his arm, he would be better off. Instead, he feels trouble coming ahead of them.

Chapter 5

What's That Feeling?

As the train is departing right on schedule at 3:40 that afternoon, Ian changes into something a little more comfortable for an eighteen hour train ride. Ian opens his travel bag and pulls out a pair of sweatpants and a shirt, nothing fancy, just relaxing. Since Ian is in a relaxing mood, he thinks he should take a short nap. As soon as Ian's head hits the pillow, he is out like a light.

Hours pass by while Ian tosses and turns on his small, lower bunk bed. It seems as if Ian still cannot shake the feeling of someone watching them at Penn Station. As he continues to toss and turn on the bed wanting to sleep, all Ian can think about is everything that has happened so far today. His dreams start off about Kenzie and how she just shows up at his apartment building, is there for about an hour, and then vanishes as quickly as she came. Literally vanishes! Kenzie not only has the gift to freeze time, but she can also transport to other places. All Ian can do is go back in time while accessing his relatives' stored moments in the Time Keeper. Even though his gift is impressive, he still feels like he is missing something.

Ian's dream then jumps to Penn Station where they boarded the train they are on now, on their way to Chicago. While Ian's memories of Penn Station feel different than when he was there earlier, he still feels like something is off, not quite right. He does not have the feeling of someone watching them this time, but it's more of a feeling of being connected to someone. He cannot figure out who he is connected to, but it feels all too real for him. Ian thinks at first maybe it is Kenzie because of their telekinetic connection, and she hasn't spoken to him in his dreams before. But Ian knows this is a different feeling. This feeling is more of a connection to his entire body and not just his mind. In the dream, he continues to look around trying to notice anything out of place. Nothing stands out to him this time, it's just like the feeling during their first visit to Penn Station.

Ian's dream suddenly takes him to Chicago. Even though he has never been to Chicago before, somehow he knows that is where he is. Standing next to Ian is a boy, just a few years older than himself, talking with some friends. He is not sure how he knows this boy is older, but he thinks to himself, *Does it really matter? It's just a dream.* The boy is about the same height as Ian, but his hair is very blond, and he has a much bigger build. The boy, with bright blue eyes, turns and looks directly at Ian and gives him a slight nod, as to acknowledge his presence, as if Ian is only visible to the boy and no one else. The boy then turns his attention back to his friends. They continue to discuss how good it is to see him, and for him not to take so long between visits from school.

Ian lets them have some privacy and begins to look around. Ian, not knowing if this is a dream, a memory, or something new altogether, decides to get some idea of what Chicago looks like. Taking in the buildings that surround them, he notices a large, kind of mirror looking, kidney shaped object sitting in the center of the park where he is standing. This made-up looking thing makes it harder for Ian to make a determination if he is dreaming or if this a real memory.

What Ian does not realize is that he is in Millennium Park, and what he is looking at is a sculpture named Cloud Gate. It was created by an Indian-born British artist named Sir Anish Kapoor who started the structure in 2004 and completed it in 2006. It was called "The Bean" because of its shape before it was finished.

It's hard to imagine that this structure is made up of 168 stainless steel plates welded together, because it's extremely polished exterior leaves no visible seams.

As Ian is staring at the Cloud Gate, he doesn't notice that the boy has turned his attention back to him. Before Ian can even try to comprehend what is going on, the boy looks directly at Ian and screams, "WAKE UP!"

Ian opens his eyes, sits up in the bed, and looks around the room, making sure he is actually awake and still on the train. Just as he finishes his initial scan of the room, Jax comes rushing in. Ian guesses that Jax must have gone to get something to eat while he was sleeping. Before Ian can inquire about Jax's whereabouts, Jax tells Ian, "Get up and get your things together as quickly as possible. We need to move, now!"

"What's going on?" Ian asks while gathering his things.

"We have been followed. I don't know how Mason found out where we were going, but he did," Jax explains to Ian.

"How do you know it's Mason?" Ian questions Jax. "Did you see him on the train?"

"No, but let's just say I have a very close friend that gave me a heads up about Mason being here. Now stop asking so many questions, and let's get a move on!"

"Where are we supposed to be going? We're on a train that is currently moving, correct?" Ian asks one last question as he is gathering his belongings. "It's not like we have a lot of options here."

"Did I say we were getting off the train?"

"No, but with our limited options, what are you planning to do, move us to the top of the train? We can't get off the train, as we have already agreed."

"Well, you are correct. We are not getting off the train but simply moving to another room. We still have thirteen hours left until we reach Chicago, so we need to get in the other room and stay out of sight," Jax instructs Ian.

"How exactly is changing rooms going to help keep us safe? Don't you think they are smart enough, and have enough time, to check every room in thirteen hours? That is unless you are planning on moving to a different room every other hour or so, which I am in no mood to do. I am too tired to keep switching rooms," Ian presses Jax for more clarification.

"Again, you are correct. We are not going to keep moving rooms. The room we are going to differs from the others on this train, and it is always only to be used as a last resort. This is one of those moments," Jax replies.

"How can it be any different than the other rooms?"

"Did you know that train tracks do not actually touch the ground? It is because of this unique way the tracks are built, which is how a special room can exist on a train. You see, train tracks are actually built on a platform to raise the track high enough to keep it from flooding. On top of that platform, the foundation is created by covering it with crushed rocks, known as ballast. Wooden beams are placed on top of the ballast perpendicular to the direction of the tracks. Once the beams are in place, they continue to put more crushed rocks all around them, since their sharp edges would keep the beams in place.

"Now that the beams are in place, the foundation for the train track is ready for the actual tracks. The hot-rolled steel rails are laid on top of the wood beams, since referred to as railroad ties. They lay the steel rails from end to end. Now, they did not nail the rails to the wood ties for several reasons. They actually attached sleepers with clips, or anchors, to the ties to hold them down. This allows for the tracks to move with the train, depending on its weight, and also keeps the tracks from changing due to the natural environments, such as ground tremors or natural weeds and undergrowth.

"This gap between the train and the earth is how we are able to create a special room that cannot be detected by others, magical or otherwise," Jax completes his explanation.

Ian finishes gathering his things, but wonders how Mason had found them. Ian barely knows where they are half of the time, much less where they are going. Ian stops thinking about Mason, for now anyway, so he can focus on making sure he leaves nothing behind. Ian already has most of his things still packed in his bag, since he went to sleep when the train began to move.

"I'm finished. What now, boss?" Ian playfully asks Jax.

"Come with me. Stay right behind me as we walk through the cars to get to the other room.

It's just a few cars down. Do not look at anyone. Just walk with your head down and follow me. You got that?" Jax scolds Ian.

I think I can handle walking with my head down. I've pretty much walked that way all my life, Ian thinks to himself while blocking out the memories of school and having to walk with his head down so the other boys would not pick on him. Those days of being bullied are behind him now, but they will always be a part of him. Now he's running from someone he doesn't even know, who is as much a bully as the other kids were in school.

As they exit their sleeper cabin and turn to the right, Ian notices the old, dingy, brown carpet in the narrow hallway. It looks as if it should have been replaced about twenty years ago. Getting past the age of the carpet, Ian can see the wood paneling that makes up the walls of the sleeper cabins. As they continue down the narrow corridor, Ian can see out of the fish tank windows on the right side of the hall. Out of the corner of his eye, he can make out the trees swishing past the windows at a good speed. While Ian is watching the trees pass by and closely following Jax, he does not notice that Jax had stopped walking, and Ian bumps right into him. Ian quickly looks up at Jax and mouths "Sorry." Jax turns back around and opens the door in front of them that connects to the next car they have to pass through, without incident this time, Jax hopes.

The door shuts behind Ian, just as he steps through it. The door closes with a slight hiss, then a locking sound. While Ian continues to walk behind Jax, his head down as required, he notices the carpet is much nicer in this car. They are no longer in a sleeper car, but more like a general sitting car. Ian can hear people talking about various things, such as what they will do when they get to Chicago, while others discuss business and other things. Ian finds none of their conversations interesting enough to continue eavesdropping on them. Just as they are about half way through this car, Ian feels a sudden, powerful need to sit down quickly in the nearest vacant seat. Ian grabs the back of Jax's shirt. As Ian falls into a seat, he pulls Jax down quickly beside him.

"What are you doing?" Jax questions Ian with surprise.

"I'm not exactly sure, Jax. Something, or someone, is telling me that we need to sit here for a few minutes. I'm not hearing voices or anything like that, but it's like an overwhelming feeling, like someone has control of my body. I don't feel like they are trying to hurt me, only to help us. I will explain more when we make it to the new room. But right now we need to act like we are sleeping," Ian quickly tells Jax. Then he immediately leans his head on the window next to his seat and shuts his eyes, while pulling his jacket over his face. Jax takes Ian's hint and leans his head back against the headrest. He places a hat over his face, which he had removed from his bag as he was being dragged down into the seat by Ian.

As they both are pretending to be sleeping, a few other passengers pass by them. Two of the passing travelers stop right beside their seats. Before Jax can react in a defensive way, one of the men begins to speak to the other one, causing Jax to hold his position as a sleeping passenger.

"We both know they are not going to be traveling out here in the general seating cars. Even if they do not know we are following them, like Mason said, they will still take precautions. They are going to be in one of the sleeper cars in a private cabin. We are wasting our time looking out here. Let's go see what information we can get from the ticket taker. He may be able to point us in a general direction if we describe the two of them to him," finishes one traveler to the other.

"Fine, let's go see what he knows," replies the other man. They stop talking and head back in the direction from where Ian and Jax had come from before taking their pretend naps.

As Jax is wondering just how long they had to "sleep," Ian leans over to Jax and tells him it is safe to continue on their way to their new room. Jax does not question Ian. He simply stands up, with Ian following suite, and they continue their walk through the passenger car. It only takes a few minutes for them to reach the next door, which is on the opposite end of the room from which they had entered. Somehow Ian knows this is the last car for them to walk through.

Ian is correct with his thinking. This is the last car for them. Jax stops at one of the sleeper cabin doors, knocks twice on it, then walks down one more door and opens it. Ian is wondering if Jax knows which room is their new one, but follows Jax through the door anyway.

Ian relaxes once he enters the room, since it is empty. Ian can't imagine what would be worse, walking into an occupied room of strangers, or walking into the occupied room of the people you were hiding from. To Ian, both would be bad.

As Ian sets his bag down on the bottom bunk bed again, he turns and looks at Jax who is giving Ian a very odd look.

"Okay, do you want to tell me what that was all about back there in the passenger car? Why did you feel the need for us to take a nap all of a sudden? And what is this about someone controlling you?" Jax is more than ready for some answers.

"Well, it's hard to explain, but I will do my best to make it simple enough for you to understand," Ian mocks Jax.

"Start talking, Ian," Jax demands.

By Jax's command, Ian explains things to him. By the look on Jax's face, he knows it will be a long conversation between the two of them.

Chapter 6

Why this Room?

As Ian finishes explaining what was happening to him in the passenger car, Jax just sits there for a minute. Jax, to Ian's surprise, has no questions, which Ian finds very strange. *How can Jax not have any questions about what just happened?* Ian cannot help but think that Jax knows more than he is telling him.

Ian holds off on trying to get more information from Jax and turns his attention back to the situation at hand. "Are we safe in this room from Mason and his goons? How long must we stay in this small room?"

"Well, Mason will not be able to find us in this room because it is a special room, remember? You see, the school has students from all over the world. For those who live in the States, the train is our choice of transportation. This room is not only used as a last resort for safety, but also for those other students who need to travel to the school. We, the teachers, do not always have the honor of meeting every student at their home. Many of the students are sent by themselves to the school, and they may, or may not, know of their powers or gifts. In order to keep them safe from others, like Mason, and to keep ordinary people safe from them as well, the school has at least one room like this one on every train. Since the room is blocked from being detected, each teacher is given a list of where the rooms are located on each train. The students who must travel alone are given instructions that will lead them to these special rooms as well. You will find out sooner or later, the school is full of very gifted and powerful young students, which we will discuss at a later time.

Since our ride is only going to be a short trip to Chicago, I requested a regular room. That way if there was another student or teacher that was traveling, they could use this special room. But as luck would have it, we are the only ones on this train today. So I was able to get our rooms switched," Jax explains to Ian.

"So, how much longer do we have to stay in this room?" Ian finishes up with his last question.

"You slept for a pretty long time, about six hours, so we only have to stay here about twelve more hours. There are plenty of things to do in this room. Remember, Ian, this is a special room. What do you have in mind to pass the time?" Jax amusingly asks Ian.

"I'm hungry. Can we order room service? I don't see a kitchen in this room, which I can assume means we cannot make our own food. So how can I get something to eat?" Ian asks Jax, pointing out the obvious.

"Who said there is no kitchen? I don't recall you asking about one or me telling you that there wasn't one. Have you looked around the room yet? I mean, really looked?" Jax replies, piquing Ian's curiosity.

As Ian looks around their new special room, nothing sticks out to him at first. But the harder he looks, the more the room changes. At first sight, the sleeper room is about the average size, three and a half feet by six and a half feet, just big enough for two adults. But as Ian trains his stare on one spot, he then can see the room is much bigger than it first appeared. Ian's eyes are now open wide, as is his mouth, with surprise. The room Ian is seeing now looks just like his apartment back home in Brooklyn. It has the same living room, kitchen, hall and even bedrooms. The only things missing are his parents. "How is this even possible? How did the school know what my home looked like?" Ian wonders out loud.

"Well, this room is special to the students who travel in it. This room is meant to make their travels more comfortable. Since many students leave home for the first time to come to our school, the room conforms to what makes them more relaxed. Now, what are you hungry for? The kitchen is fully stocked with everything you like," Jax finishes.

Ian doesn't even answer Jax's question. He has already starting walking into the kitchen. Ian has not had time to think about what he is hungry for, so he opens the cabinets until he finds a snack for now. Ian settles on a microwavable bowl of macaroni and cheese and an individual pouch of tuna fish. Ian removes the cover off the mac and cheese, fills the water to the fill line, and places it in the microwave for three and a half minutes. While his bowl of noodles is cooking, Ian rips open the top of the pouch of tuna fish. Taking a fork from one of the kitchen drawers, Ian scrapes the fork all around the inside of the pouch of tuna fish to break it up. Just as he finishes breaking up the tuna, the microwave bell sounds. Ian removes the bowl of freshly boiled noodles, tears open the pouch that contains the cheese for the noodles, and squeezes the contents into the bowl of hot noodles. After Ian is finished mixing the noodles and cheese, he adds the pouch of tuna fish, and mixes the three ingredients together. Once they are all combined to his liking, he grabs a bottle of water from the refrigerator and heads back into the living room. Ian is ready to enjoy one of his favorite snacks. Ian takes a seat on the couch that was once used to tie down Jax, so he wouldn't float away after Kenzie had frozen time. Ian sets his water down on the end table and munches down on his easy dinner.

"What in the world are you eating?" Jax inquires.

"Mac and cheese with tuna fish. My mom used to make this for me when I was little. It may not sound good, but it is the best!" Ian exclaims. Ian is very relaxed being on a train in a room that looks like his home and eating his favorite food from home. Things can't get better than this for Ian.

"Well, while you eat and get comfortable, I'm going to make a few calls. I need to check in with Brayden and make sure he will be at the station on time. We will have a four hour layover in Chicago until we board the Texas Eagle 421 for the next leg of our travels. I also need to inform Brayden about Mason being on the train, so he can be extra cautious when he does arrive. Since Chicago Union Station is so open, I will make contact with a former student of mine to let us gain access to the Legacy Club. It has a special room there as well. Just in case Mason checks for us at the station, we will be safe there at the club. It should only take me about an hour to make my calls. Just stay in this room, and don't open the door for any reason, understand?"

Ian just sits there eating his snack, and nods his head back at Jax. Ian takes his time finishing this meal, but to his surprise he is already full.

After cleaning up the mess he made from cooking his dinner and eating, Ian sits and looks out of the window. Everything looks so beautiful whisking by the window as the train moves westward. Between the motion of the train and the passing colors in the window, Ian falls asleep again. Ian lays his head down on the window sill and lets his mind and body rest. He doesn't want to dream. He wants to rest, and so he does.

***

"Hey, Kayla, where have you been? I have been looking everywhere for you," Ian asks when he first sees Kayla standing next to his bed.

"What are you talking about? I went shopping with my mom," Kayla replies. "Now get up and get ready, or we are going to be late."

"Late for what?"

"Oh, stop with all these crazy questions and get ready. I'll wait for you in the living room," Kayla responds with a smile.

Kayla turns around and walks out of Ian's room, closing his bedroom door behind her.

Ian does what Kayla asks of him and gets out of bed to get ready. Ready for what, he is still unsure of, but nonetheless he is going to be ready. Ian gathers his clothes for the day and walks over to his bedroom door. He grabs the doorknob and gives it a turn, pulls it open, and walks out of his room to go get ready in the bathroom down the hall.

To Ian's surprise, as he exits his room, he is already dressed and ready for the day. He hears Kayla calling from the living room, "It's about time."

He makes his way down the hallway and to the living room where he finds Kayla standing next to Michael.

"Surprise!" Both Kayla and Michael shout at the exact same time.

"What are you both doing here? Why are you both shouting at me, and what's the surprise?" Ian asks them both nervously.

"What are you talking about, Ian? It's just me here. Is everything alright with you?" They both reply again at the same time.

"Why are you and Michael both here in my living room? What is this surprise we are going to be late for?" Ian asks, at this point to either of them.

"Stop playing around, Ian. You know we have to go, and you know why," they reply again together.

"You have not answered my question yet. Why are you both here?" he asks one more time. But before Ian's question can be answered, Kayla and Michael begin to merge into each other right in front of him. Everything happens so fast, and before Ian can react, he sees that it is only Michael, of the original two, left standing in front of him.

"Are you ready to go? You know we can't be late. How often do we get invited to something like this?" Michael is asking Ian.

"What just happened? Where did Kayla go? What are you doing here? What are we invited to?" Ian is freaking out now.

"Who is Kayla? What is wrong with you, man? We have to leave now, or we are going to be late. Now, whatever is going on with you right now, you need to get ahold of yourself. We can't be late," Michael finishes as he is walking to the living room door which leads to the hallway.

Ian's mind is spinning is every direction right now, but he follows Michael to the door. Michael turns the knob and opens the door. As Ian is the last one out, he closes the front door. But when he turns back to ask Michael where they are going, he notices Michael is not moving.

"Michael, are you okay? What's wrong? Why are you standing there?" Ian asks.

Michael does not reply. He is frozen in time. This is when Ian recalls meeting Kenzie for the first time. *What is going on?*

"Kenzie? Are you here?" Ian whispers, as he is not wanting to draw attention from his neighbors. "You can come out. You are safe here."

All of a sudden, a little girl comes out from the stairwell. Ian recognizes her immediately. It's Kenzie.

"How do you know my name?" the little girl asks Ian.

"What do you mean? It's me, Ian. Don't you remember me? You came here earlier today by accident. You teleported here and then you teleported back home to your parents," Ian explains.

"We called them to make sure you made it home safely. And they said you were there. Don't you remember any of this?" Ian has a bit of concern in his voice.

"I don't have any parents. My parents died in a car accident when I was very little. Why would you bring them up? That's so cruel," Kenzie replies to Ian with a hint of sadness.

"I'm sorry. I didn't know that about your parents. If your parents died, then who do you live with now? Who did we call earlier?" Ian finishes.

"What do you mean you called earlier? Who did you call?" Kenzie is full of questions as well. "I don't know who I am living with. I don't even know anything about myself, so why don't you just stop asking me all of these questions?"

"Well, Jax and I thought we called your parents earlier after you teleported here and then vanished. Before you vanished, you gave Jax your phone number, so he could call them to let them know you were safe. Don't you remember any of this?" Ian is still unsure of what is happening.

Am I reliving this or is the past changing? Ian thinks to himself.

"What does it matter **what** this is? It's too late anyway. I have to go now, before he finds me. Don't come looking for me, because this is all your fault!" Kenzie commands as she vanishes from Ian's sight, again.

Next thing Ian knows, Michael is unfrozen and speaking, "This is all your fault, Ian," Michael says to Ian as they are standing in the hall.

What is my fault? Ian thinks to himself as he turns around and grabs the front door to his apartment, pushes it open and rushes in, slamming the door shut behind him before Michael can get in.

As he turns away from the door, he sees he is back in his bedroom, not the living room. He notices Kayla is standing there talking to him, except he is lying on the bed. He is now watching a conversation between himself and Kayla.

"This is all your fault. You created all of this and did this to all of us. Why did you do this to us, Ian?" Kayla is yelling at the Ian laying on the bed.

"What's my fault? What do you mean I did this to all of you? What did I do to you all?" The Ian on the bed is now sitting up and responding to Kayla.

Kayla, standing between the two Ians, the one sitting on the bed and the one that just entered the room standing at the bedroom door, turns her head and is staring at the Ian at the door now. With her eyes dark as night, she opens her mouth and just starts screaming, "YOU DID THIS! DON'T EVER FORGET IT!"

The Ian at the door is struck with fear. Fear he has never felt from Kayla before. *What did I do to cause all of this?* But before he could think of a reply back to himself, he hears his name being called.

"Ian! Ian!" This is a familiar voice, but one he has not heard yet in this dream. "Ian, it's time to wake up."

It's Jax waking Ian from his sleep.

Ian wanted to be able to sleep and just dream, but this is not what he was expecting.

Chapter 7

What is Real Anymore?

"Ian, it's time to get up. You have been asleep for ten hours," Jax tells Ian as he is tapping Ian on his shoulder.

Between the rocking of the train and Jax's tapping, Ian begins to slowly wake up. Ian was in such a deep sleep, and with waking up in a train cabin identical to his home, he almost forgot where he was. But when he looks up and sees Jax, he quickly remembers.

"What do you mean I have been asleep for ten hours? Are you combining the hours I slept from before with this time?" Ian asks Jax.

"No, Ian. You have been asleep for another ten straight hours. I am starting to worry about you. What has gotten into you to make you sleep this much? What were you dreaming about, or what did you see?" Jax inquiries from Ian.

"I'm not sure what is going on, or if anything is. I think it is just being on the train that makes me sleepy. Something about the rocking of the train and the sounds of the trees whooshing by, made it easy for me to fall asleep. Is there anything wrong with me getting rest?" Ian questions Jax.

"No, there is nothing wrong with you getting rest, except that I have been trying to wake you for over four hours. No matter what I did, you would not wake up. It was like you were stuck in some loop, or in some memory. I was beginning to worry until you finally woke up just now," Jax expresses to Ian.

"How much longer do we have to ride this train until we are in Chicago?" Ian questions Jax.

"Well, since you have slept for so long, you have about thirty minutes to get up, get a shower, and get ready to disembark. We are almost there," Jax replies.

Ian gets up from the window sill where he had fallen asleep earlier, goes to his room, gathers the things he needs, and heads to the bathroom to get ready to meet this new student, Brayden. Once Ian is in the bathroom, he turns on the shower to let the water warm before getting in. As the shower is warming up, Ian undresses and then steps into the steamy shower. Ian stands under the warm water that is running down over his head, shoulders, back, and all the way down to his feet. Ian feels all he has been doing is running the past few days, sweating and picking up dirt from everything and everyone with whom he came into contact. While the water continues to wash away Ian's days, he shampoos his hair nice and good, then gives it a good rinse. After his hair is clean, he soaps up his body, which helps release the dirt he has accumulated. Ian feels so much better and cleaner now that he is finishing rinsing all the dirty, soapy water away. After turning off the water, Ian grabs his towel to dry off. Ian dries his hair first, then his face, then the rest of his freshly cleaned body.

Ian steps out of the shower and positions himself in front of the bathroom sink and mirror. The mirror is foggy from the steamy shower, so Ian reaches for a dry hand towel to wipe off the mirror to get a better look at himself. As he wipes off the mist from the mirror, he sees something which is not his own reflection. Ian continues to wipe off the mirror until the image is more visible to him. To Ian's surprise, he can tell he is seeing

Kenzie. She is lying on the floor of some strange room. *Is this real?* Ian wonders to himself.

"Kenzie!" Ian shouts at the vision in the mirror, but there is no reply. "Kenzie, can you hear me?" Ian yells louder this time while knocking on the mirror. On his third knock, his hand goes straight through the mirror. Surprisingly, his hand does not break the mirror, but simply goes directly into it. As his hand enters through the mirror, he feels something hit his hand on the other side. Then he hears something breaking. He must have knocked something over on the other side of the mirror. As he quickly pulls his hand back out of the mirror, he sees Kenzie jump up out of her sleep and look around the room. *Did I break something in the room where Kenzie is?* Ian asks himself, not knowing what to think. Just as Kenzie looks in Ian's direction, she has a surprised look on her face. As the image in the mirror of Kenzie starts coming closer towards Ian, the vision suddenly vanishes.

Once Kenzie is gone from the mirror, Ian tries knocking on it again but nothing happens. Still unsure what to believe, Ian grabs the same hand towel he used to wipe the mirror the first time and gives it another cleaning. After setting the towel down, Ian stares into the mirror while thinking of Kenzie as hard as he can. But again nothing changes. He can only see his own reflection staring back at him. *How did I do that?* He wonders. Then he is snapped back to reality by Jax knocking on the bathroom door. Ian decides he is not going to tell Jax about his interactions with Kenzie through the mirror, not yet at least.

"Ian, are you about ready? The train is about to pull into the station," Jax informs Ian.

Ian doesn't reply to Jax. He just opens the bathroom door and walks out of the bathroom, all dressed for the day with all of his toiletries in his hand. This is the only hint Jax needs to know that Ian is ready to leave the train.

"Now, we need to get off the train with the rest of the passengers. That way we can use them as cover from Mason. Brayden is going to meet us at the Legacy Club. We need to walk with our heads down, but not too fast. We do not want to draw any undue attention to ourselves. Once we are out in the open, we are going to be an easy target for Mason and his goons, understand?" Jax instructs Ian.

As the train comes to a complete stop, Ian and Jax wait for a group of people to exit the train before them. The duo then exits between the first group and a second group. They make their way from the platform, to the luggage area, past the luggage carousel, and head straight towards the back to the great hall.

The pair make their way past the Amtrak Metropolitan Lounge in order to arrive at their destination, the Legacy Club. As soon as they walk in through the doors of the club, they are met by a young employee, Sam. He is a graduate student from the school Ian is going to attend. Sam leads Ian and Jax down a small corridor between the restroom doors until they reach their private room. As soon as Sam opens the door to their private room, they can see Brayden is not there yet. Jax does not look too happy about being the first to arrive, but he does not voice that out loud to Ian. Jax will deal with Brayden after he and Ian get settled in the room.

***

Still locked in the basement by the charlatan, Kenzie stands in front of the mirror for fifteen minutes after Ian vanishes. She calls his name several times, but Ian's image does not return. As far as Kenzie knows, she did not make this happen. She could not, since she was asleep until Ian's hand came through the mirror and knocked over the picture frame that is now on the floor.

Kenzie bends down to pick up the broken picture frame before her abductor comes into the room. As she picks up the broken glass, wooden frame, and the photo that had fallen out, she spots some writing on the back of the photo. Kenzie places the photo in her pocket and discards the broken glass and frame into the wastebasket. Just as she is walking back over to the mirror, the basement door bursts open.

The woman who has been pretending to be Kenzie's mother comes into the room. The woman doesn't have enough time to make it down the basement stairs before Kenzie is already on the move from the dresser with the mirror over to the couch. The last thing she wants is for her captors to gain any more knowledge about Ian, or his powers, than they may possibly already know. Kenzie moves as fast as she can and makes it to the sofa just before the woman makes it past the last two steps and into the room.

"What was that noise I heard coming from down here?" the woman angrily asks.

"I'm not sure what noise you are speaking about. Can you describe what you think you may have heard?" Kenzie replies back, not wanting to reveal more than is necessary.

"Well, the sound of something breaking, and you saying something, very loudly I might add," the woman inquires.

"Oh, that. Well, that was me knocking the lamp off the end table accidentally. You see, I was having this horrible nightmare. I was dreaming I was being held against my will by these evil people from some other time in space. For some reason they were keeping me locked in a basement of some sort. Then I woke up and remembered something very important." Kenzie pauses for some dramatic effects, "What was it again? Oh, yes, now I remember. It was that I am **not** in a dream at all," Kenzie smiles really big at her. "As you can see, it did fall over, but it did not break. Sorry if I am disturbing you up there while I am down here locked in this basement. I will try to be more of a quiet prisoner for you," Kenzie mockingly explains. "If you don't mind, I would rather be alone right now."

Without another word, the woman turns and goes back up the stairs leading out of the basement, leaving Kenzie alone again. But for how long, Kenzie is unsure.

Saving History – School Bound

Once she hears the door to the basement lock, Kenzie takes a deep breath to try and slow her heart rate. Now that she has her composure back, she gets up off the couch and makes her way over to the dresser. She is not sure what she expects to see, if anything, but she still feels the need to inspect everything on the dresser. Kenzie takes a moment to touch the mirror and see if she is able to put her hand through it, but with no luck. She looks over the mirror and dresser until she is sure she is completely alone. Not even Ian is there with her.

***

Ian has never been in a private club before, especially not one like the Legacy Club. This is a place like no other at the train station, from what he has read about it. Their private room is fairly large for just the two of them. The walls are lined with red velvet curtains that hang from the ceiling down to the floor. The room's furnishings are a plush, black couch and chair, both with high backs, and just a few tables. The furniture reminds Ian of pieces he could have found in the king's castle. The one from the memory he was shown, when he was eighteen. As Ian is taking in the beauty of the room, Jax is on the phone with Brayden. *Nothing like a loud phone conversation to ruin the mood*, Ian thinks to himself.

Jax finishes his call to Brayden and walks over to Ian to fill him in on what's going on.

"Well, Brayden won't be too much longer. He decided to take a few additional precautions just to make sure he is not followed here. Is there anything you want to do, or eat, while we wait?" Jax asks Ian.

"No, I'm good thanks," replies Ian.

Jax shakes his head at Ian, turns around, and walks over to the oversized round wooden table which sits in the center of the room. Jax grabs a seat at the table and reads a newspaper that has been left there.

About twenty minutes after Jax takes a seat at the table, the sound of the door opening makes them both jump. They both have the same fearful thought that maybe Mason has found them. They each take defensive positions in the room. To their surprise, and relief, it is only Brayden who enters.

As Brayden walks into the room, he is carrying a small duffle bag and wearing a green and black backpack. Then Ian notices Brayden's blue eyes, blond hair, and muscular build. Ian knows he has seen this boy before.

"It's you!" Ian exclaims. "You are the one that told me to wake up. You were in my dream."

"You must be Ian," Brayden replies. "Yes, I was in your dream, but I was not in control of my actions in your dream. I was not the one who told you to wake up. It was someone else. I can't explain it, but it was like someone was controlling me, making me shout to you to wake up," Brayden tries to explain to Ian.

"That's what was happening to me after I woke up. I could feel someone in control over my whole mind and body. They knew things were going to happen before they happened. Whoever it is, I don't think they want to harm us, but to help us," Ian tells Jax and Brayden.

"Okay, now this is something we need to figure out, but now is not the time. We need to get to our next train without being seen by Mason or his men," Jax interjects. "We have about an hour to create a plan on how we are going to achieve our goal. Do either of you have any suggestions?"

The three spend the entire next hour shooting out suggestions. They seem to settle on a plan, but they still have their doubts that it will work. But time is almost up, so it is now or never. They need to get a move on if their plan is going to succeed. The three gather up their belongings and head to the door to leave the private room just as Sam comes walking into the room.

Sam informs them there have been no signs of Mason or his men. Now that does not mean it is safe for them, it just means Mason is also taking precautions. All is not lost, as Sam informs them there is a private walkway to the train platform they can take. From there, they can load onto the train and not be seen by anyone. This comes as a great relief, since they all had doubts about the plan they had come up with anyway.

Sam walks over to the wall directly behind the beautiful black, king couch and moves the red velvet curtains over to one side revealing a hidden door. This is the private passageway to the train platform Sam had told them about. Sam opens the door and leads them to the end of the passageway, before stopping.

The fact that Sam once was a student of Jax's, reminds him just how smart Sam is with this plan. Sam gives them instructions on getting on the train and to their room without being seen, says his goodbyes, and heads back down the passageway, back to his position in the Legacy

Club. Sam explains that it will look less suspicious if he is seen leaving the main entrance to the Legacy room alone, just in case anyone from Mason's group is watching the room.

Robert Starnes

Chapter 8

Who's in Control?

Jax, Brayden, and Ian remain at the end of the secret passageway they have taken from the Legacy Club. They stay where they are until their train arrives, the 21 Texas Eagle.

As the train pulls up, Ian feels excitement about this leg of his journey. The 21 Texas Eagle is the next to the last train they will have to take until they reach the school in Houston. Ian is determined to get some answers to his many questions, not only from Jax, but now from Brayden as well. Ian knows he has about seventeen hours before they reach San Antonio to ask Jax and Brayden all of his questions.

Once the train comes to a full stop, they wait until the platform is full of passengers loading and unloading before they make their move onto the train. There are travelers coming and going from all directions. It is easier for them to blend in with groups of travelers than it is trying to board the train as a lone trio, cautiously looking out for Mason. It is going to be hard to spot Mason or his men, since Jax is the only one that knows what Mason looks like.

With a full platform, Jax takes the lead and heads into a group that is passing in front of them. Jax makes sure the three of them are all in the same group together and walking at an even pace towards the train entrance. To Ian, it feels as if they are walking in an open field with large targets strapped to their backs. This feeling starts to make Ian anxious.

Ian's anxiety is rising and starting to fill his mind with paranoia, because he is afraid of crowded or small places. He begins to look around in a panic. The only thing he is thinking about is when he was left in his school locker by Michael, in middle school. Something so childish has stuck with Ian his entire life and caused this anxiety. Before he has a full panic attack, a hand on his shoulder catches his attention. It is Jax. Jax's hand on his shoulder brings Ian's anxiety level down enough for him to see they are already at the train door.

Now that they have successfully used the crowd to blend in enough to make it to the door of the nearest passenger car, and with Jax's hand on his shoulder, Ian feels a little less tense. Ian knows Mason's men are looking for them, but he is also worrying about Kenzie.

The three board the train with no problem. Jax leads them to their "special room." Jax guides them through a passenger car and one other sleeper car, until they reach their private room. Jax knocks on the door with three short knocks, then the door unlocks. Jax grabs the door handle and gives the door a slight push while turning the handle. The door opens with such ease.

As they enter the room, Ian notices that it does not resemble his home like the last one did on their train to Chicago. This room is just another sleeper car, except it has three beds along one wall, bunk beds, each one above the other, instead of just two. As Ian makes his way into the room, he drops his bag down on the bottom bed, just as he did before. Brayden has taken the top bunk, leaving the middle for Jax. Ian isn't too worried about Jax sleeping above him, as he figures Jax sleeps very little anyway. Jax has taken on the role of their protector, always watching and making plans in his mind, preparing for anything that could come up. Ian has no problem sleeping, knowing he is safe. As Ian takes his place on his bed, he can hear Jax questioning Brayden about his tardiness to the Legacy Club. As Ian listens, he slowly blocks their voices and once again he drifts off to sleep.

While Ian is sleeping, Jax and Brayden continue to catch up on all the events that have happened to all three of them. When they finish, Jax goes to take a walk around the train. He wants to see if anything unusual is going on.

After Jax closes the door behind him, Brayden has this sudden feeling to walk over and wake Ian up again. Being unable to control his body, the next thing he knows he is sitting on Ian's bed, shaking him softly trying to wake him. As Ian comes to, he has a surprised look on his face. He is not expecting Brayden to be waking him.

"What do you want?" Ian asks Brayden.

"You are safe from this point until you reach Houston. Mason knows where you are going, so he will not make another move until you reach the city," Brayden replies to Ian.

"How do you know all of this? I don't remember any texts or calls from Mason saying he is just going to wait—" Ian breaks off as Brayden interrupts him.

"Trust me, Ian. I know more than you think. I have been watching you since you left for Chicago. With Brayden's abilities, it is easier for me to communicate directly to you through him," Brayden finishes.

"Who are you? How do you know all of this? How do you know what Mason has planned?" Ian spits out his questions.

"In time, you will have all your questions answered, but not right now. I will do my very best to make sure you three make it to the school safely. I have to go for now. If Mason catches me communicating with you, he may realize what I have been doing, which could end up being a very bad thing. I'm sorry, Ian. I never meant to put you, or anyone else, in danger by contacting you. But I was left with no other options," are the final words from Brayden's mouth. Brayden came to and realized that "it" happened to him again.

"Do you remember any of what just happened?" Ian asks Brayden.

"Yes, I remember all of it. That is the same person that took over my body in your dream. I can feel them taking over, and whoever they are, they are very strong. Their powers are much greater than mine," Brayden explains to Ian. "They do seem to know you personally though."

"Why would you say that?" Ian questions.

"Because, when they are talking through me, they are talking to you. I can feel their emotions when I am speaking for them. They feel very strongly towards you. Also, at the end, they apologized to you for not telling you about them," Brayden retorts.

Ian has not had time to break down the conversation he just had with the person controlling Brayden. Ian thought he was talking to Brayden at first, so he wasn't playing close attention to the words. Once he realized it was not Brayden speaking, he was in shock and tried to comprehend the rest of the conversation. Now that Brayden is back in control of himself, Ian asks Brayden if he can repeat the message again.

Brayden recalls the message as precisely as he can. Ian listens to the words this time, then he also believes this is someone he knows. The only problem is, Ian has no clue who it could be. Some good news did come from the message and that is that they are safe for the rest of the trip, at least until they reach Houston. This will give them time to get to know each other a little better.

By the time they finish talking about the message, Jax comes walking into the room.

"Well, so far everything looks okay. I didn't see any sign of Mason or his men," Jax assures them both.

"We know," Ian replies. "While you were out checking the train, we had a message delivered to us. The person who has been taking control over our minds and bodies took over Brayden's body to give me a message. They said we are going to be safe, at least until we make it to Houston. They said that Mason knows where we are headed, so he decided to wait until we get there," explains Ian. "Why would they tell us that if they didn't want to help us? Whoever it is risked a lot to get that message to us when they didn't have to do it. They didn't have to tell us anything, and we would be on edge, sleep deprived, and extremely stressed by the time we did run into Mason, or his foot soldiers," Ian conveys to Jax.

"That seems convenient, doesn't it? How do you know this is not a trick to get us to let our guard down so they can attack?" Jax questions.

"I know that this may sound strange, but I trust them, whoever they are. They have already helped us twice, once in my dream about Brayden and the other when we were walking through the passenger car on our way to Chicago. Also, they know me. I don't know how they know me, or who they are, but they are trying to help," Ian says, hoping to reassure Jax.

Brayden agrees with Ian, by explaining to Jax the feeling he felt from the person that took control of his body.

Even though they both make compelling arguments that this person is a friend, Jax still will not let his guard down. Jax will continue to check the train and their surroundings until they make it to the school where he knows they will be safe for sure.

**

"Why are you doing this to Ian?" she asks her captor.

"Simple, I need Ian to access a memory that is stored in the Time Keeper. I need him to take me back to fix a terrible wrong that was committed, and I can't just force him to do it. Therefore, I will need you to make sure it happens," Mason informs his prisoner.

**

Previously when Mason meets Kayla for the first time, they speak for a few minutes, until she tells him she needs to take a hot bath due to her headache. He agrees to her having a bath, and then he continues back to the control room. He knows that Alexis is hiding something from him about Kayla, and he needs to know what.

As Kayla is left in the bathroom for her hot bath, she is given instructions to press the intercom when she is ready to be escorted back to her room. It's too bad she does not know Mason is able to listen in the room even without her pressing the button. What he overhears is astonishing.

At first he is unsure what to think since he is only able to listen in on a conversation Kayla is having with herself. He can only hear her words and is unable to see into the room. He is unable to make heads or tails of what he is hearing. Kayla is speaking of Alexis wiping her memories, or adding fakes one. Then there is something about her being erased from history, which Mason knows Kayla has something to do with the Time Keeper. Now the last part is what really catches his attention. Kayla can contact Ian, but she has been instructed not to by Alexis. "Now how can she contact him?" Mason questions out loud to no one in particular.

Mason waits until she has completed her bath and presses the intercom to signal she is ready to head back to her room, before he heads to her room himself. Mason is already present when she arrives back with the nurse from the bathroom.

After the nurse leaves, Kayla and Mason exchange a few words, and he leaves her alone to eat the food he has ordered for her. He still needs to know how she can contact Ian. So he takes a stance outside of her door. Mason does not move from his position until he hears Kayla speaking. All he hears is, "Don't forget me, Ian," from Kayla.

Hearing those words, he quickly opens her bedroom door to catch her communicating with Ian. But what he finds is a sleeping Kayla. That is when he is able to put it all together. They have a telepathic connection. *That is why Alexis was able to erase and plant memories in Kayla's mind. That is how I will get Ian to do what I need him to do for me, through her.* Mason walks away knowing more than Alexis thought he would.

***

"What makes you so sure he will do it for me? I have already removed myself from his history," she replies. She is careful to leave out the part that, even though she removed herself from Ian's history, he is the only person who remembers her. Kayla is counting on his memories of her staying in tack, until she can figure out how she can be put back in current time.

"Like I said, I can't force him to take me back to the past, but maybe you can actually do it for him. Since he doesn't remember you, then he won't suspect its coming, now will he?" Mason says with certainty.

Kayla shutters thinking about what Mason could mean by those words, to complete Mason's mission.

Chapter 9

Who are You?

As the others are making their way closer to Houston, Kenzie is trying to figure out how to access her gifts. She has been locked in the basement for most of the day, and so far she has been unable to freeze time or teleport more than a few feet. Her growing concerns now are who this Mason person is, and what he has to do with everything. She knows he is the leader of the group her parents, using phrase lightly, are a part of, but what is it that he is needing with her?

Taking a break from trying to use her powers, Kenzie thinks now is a good time to get some answers from her captors. Kenzie figures her fake father should be home by now, so she walks up the basement stairs and knocks on the locked door which leads to the upper part of the house. To her surprise, it is Connor, her little brother, who is opening the door for her. *Why is it that he is not locked in a room? Is it because he does not have any powers?* She wonders many things about Connor, about if he is her real brother or not, about if he has any powers, but she is happy nonetheless to see him and know he is safe.

"Connor, are you okay?" Kenzie asks with great concern.

"Yes, why wouldn't I be?" he replies.

"It's a long story. Where are your, I mean, our parents?" Kenzie inquires, almost forgetting Connor may not know what she knows of their so-called parents.

"They are in the front sitting room with their friend," Connor tells her.

"What friend?"

"His name is Mr. Mason, I think."

Just as Kenzie is about to grab Connor and run for the back door, their "father" enters the room. This is the first time Kenzie has been face to face with him since learning of the lies about them being their parents. She is filled with anger, but remembers she is unable to freeze him and does not want to take a chance on scaring or hurting Connor. So she does nothing.

"And where do you think you are going?" he asks.

"We are heading to the front room to join you," Kenzie tells him, not wanting to say anything that may frighten her little brother.

"Connor, go up to your room while we have a talk with your sister," requests his father.

Without a word, Connor turns and walks to his room.

Now that Connor is out of the room, the man forcefully grabs Kenzie by the arm and leads her into the front room where her fake mother and Mason are waiting. As she is being dragged to the other room, Kenzie wonders, *What do they want from me?*

When the pair enter the front sitting room, Mason, Kenzie presumes, is already standing. As Kenzie is being led to the couch, she is searching her memories for this Mason person, but she draws a blank. Kenzie knows she has never seen this man before. *How does this man know me?* Kenzie thinks to herself. She takes a seat on the sofa, as if she has a choice.

"It is so nice to finally meet you, Kenzie. Your mother and father were just filling me in on the events of the day. So, how was your first trip to Brooklyn?" Mason sarcastically asks.

"What are you talking about?" Kenzie replies, as if she doesn't know what he is talking about.

"Don't worry. I have already told your parents about where you were and what you can do," Mason informs her with a very smug tone. "There is no need to act like you don't know what I'm talking about. There is nothing you, or the others, can do without my knowing about it," Mason lectures Kenzie.

"You see, I have been watching you all for a very long time. I know about all of your powers, or gifts, as you call them. I have been planning this for many years. Just ask your parents. They will tell you," Mason finishes.

"Please, stop calling them my parents. We both know they are not my or Connor's real parents," Kenzie spits at Mason. "You know Connor and I were given to these people as payment for something they did for you."

"Well, it seems you have been filled in as well," Mason snaps back at Kenzie while giving the mother a sharp look. "Very well, it's true. Jerry and Delores did do something for me years ago. As payment for the completion of their assignment and for their loyalty, I gave them what they desired most, a family. I chose to let them raise you and Connor. It was the least I could do for them.

See, your real parents were a part of our group before you were born. When your parents found out that your real mother was with child, they removed themselves from our group. They began to feel that my plans for all of us were not something they could be a part of anymore. They did a fairly good job of hiding from us. But after only a year of searching, I found them, and you. After I confronted them and gave them the choice of living without you or something bad happening to them, they chose the former of the two options and gave you to me." Mason seems to enjoy telling this story. Kenzie can see it in his eyes.

"Now you see why I say your parents didn't deserve to raise such a special child as yourself. Truly loving parents would die for their children. Yet your parents chose not to fight," Delores explains her previous comment to Kenzie while looking pleased with herself.

"Alright, enough small talk. Why are you still here, Kenzie? We know you have the power to teleport, so why haven't you gone?" Mason inquires.

"Who says I've been here this whole time? How do you know that I didn't leave again and come back?" remarks Kenzie.

"Remember, I have ways of knowing what you have or haven't done. I know you have not left this house since your return from Brooklyn. Can it be that you have not figured out how to use your teleportation, *yet*?" Mason spits out the last word as if it is something she should have already mastered.

Kenzie, not wanting to confirm his suspicions, replies, "I have chosen to stay around because of Connor. If you know everything about me, then you should know that I will not leave without my brother."

"Would that change if I told you that Connor is not your brother?" Mason asks.

Kenzie could not respond, not right away anyway, after hearing these words. *Connor is not my brother?* She thinks to herself. If this were true, she knows that it will not change the use of her powers, so she replies, "No, it would not change anything. Connor, to me, is my brother no matter what you say." Kenzie feels these words to be true in her heart. Kenzie knows she must save, not only herself, but also Connor.

As Mason does not reply to her answer, Kenzie is worried about how she can save them both. She still does not understand how to activate her teleportation, much less know if she can take someone with her. While she worries, Mason has been watching her long enough to know she is telling him the truth about Connor.

Wanting to move the conversation away from Connor and her real parents and back to the matter at hand, Mason speaks to them all. "I believe you, Kenzie. As long as you do as I instruct you to do, when I instruct you to do it, neither you nor Connor will be harmed. Now, no more questions. Think about that while you are down in the basement." While looking over at Delores, Mason firmly demands, "Remove her from my sight!"

Delores takes the responsibility of making sure Kenzie makes it back to the basement, since Mason was looking at her when he gave the order to remove the girl. Kenzie goes willingly, knowing she needs time to figure out how she can save them both, Connor and herself. Delores opens the basement door, and as Kenzie makes her way through it, she hears Mason tell Jerry, "Now, bring me the boy."

As Mason finishes speaking those words, before Kenzie has a chance to react, Delores shuts the basement door and locks it. Kenzie finds herself struck with a sudden rush of fear. Memories of Connor shoot through her mind, and she can feel energy building inside her. It seems the more she thinks about Connor being near Mason, the more energy she feels building up. Just when she felt she was going to scream from all the bottled up energy, she is gone.

Kenzie vanishes from the basement of her fake parents' house in a flash.

***

Connor hates being told what to do all the time, especially when his parents have company, like Mr. Mason. This time he is not allowed to go play outside, but ordered to his room.

Connor can think of nothing more than wanting to be outside, but for some reason he is being told to stay in his room today. He is not sure what, if anything, he has done for him to be grounded. *What did I do?* Connor wonders. He closes his bedroom door behind him as he enters his room, following his father's orders.

Connor decides since he will not be enjoying the outside today, he will remain in his onesie pajamas. They are the ones with the race cars on them. *What's the point of getting clean and dressed if I have to stay in my room all day?* He questions himself.

Not knowing how long he is going to be in his room today, Connor sits on his bedroom floor and starts to play with the toys that are already there. He knows he is supposed to pick up his toys after he is through playing with them and put them back in his toy box, but last night he left them out. Not only has he left his toys on the floor, but there are more toys at the foot of his bed. His bed, which is shaped like a race car to match his pajamas, has plenty of space at the foot of it since he is not tall enough yet to reach the end.

While Connor is alone in his room, he is not paying much attention to what is going on downstairs. Connor enjoys playing with his toys alone, this way Kenzie doesn't mess with them. Now, he has no problem messing with Kenzie when she is playing with her dolls, but to him this is different. He thinks all little brothers should be able to bother their big sisters, but not the other way around.

Connor has been playing with his Bumble Bee Transformer for the last fifteen minutes and is growing bored with it. He looks over at his overstuffed toy box that is under his bedroom window. The toy box is overflowing with even more toys. As he is looking at his toy box, all he can think of is his Captain America action figure. He reaches his arms out towards the toy box, and the box starts to move and rattle. The toys in the box are shuffling around to make room for the Captain to be free. Captain America must have been on the bottom of the toy box, because it takes a minute for him to make it out of the box. Once the Captain is free, he begins to float across the room until he reaches Connor's hands.

He has the Captain firmly in his grasp, but before he can start to play with his new toy, he hears Kenzie's voice saying, "NOW!" Unsure what to make of hearing her voice, he goes back to playing with his favorite Avenger, Captain America.

Before Connor knows it, the mirror on his dresser starts to shake. The first thing he thinks of is, *Is that me? Because if it's not me, I don't want anyone to see what I just did. I don't want people to think that I'm different.* In an attempt to pretend nothing happened, he just stops what he is doing and waits, while remaining calm. What happens next is not something he is prepared for.

Chapter 10

How did this Happen?

Jax continues his overprotecting watch for the three travelers, leaving Brayden and Ian time alone to get to know more about each other.

"So, how long have you been going to the school?" Ian asks Brayden.

"Well, my parents sent me to the school when they first learned of my powers. I was eight."

"Where you scared?"

"Scared of what? Finding out I have powers or that my parents were sending me away because of them?" Brayden asks Ian for a more specific line of questioning.

"I'm sorry. I didn't realize—" Ian is cut off by Brayden.

"I'm just kidding with you, dude. I was eight years old, so of course I was scared. I did not know what I did to activate my powers. But my parents knew that day would come, so they were prepared for it.

My parents sent me away to the school so I could learn how to use my powers and also learn the history of them. They also sent me there for my own protection. They realized then that if others knew I was different from them, they could try to hurt me. You see, people are scared of what they are not a part of and what they don't understand. People without powers are scared of those of us with powers, because they do not know what it is like to be the one with these gifts. They don't know how it feels. It's like a burden sometimes, being different from everyone else. The school is a place where we can be who were are born to be, without fear," Brayden explains.

"Just how many others out there in the world have these gifts? Are there a lot of different powers students have at the school?" Ian has a ton of questions for Brayden.

"Slow down there, buddy. There are many different types of people with different types of powers in the world, but they are just like everyone else. They are still just people.

Saving History – School Bound

Now you will find out at the school that not all of the students are there on the happiest of terms. Many of them were born with their powers, but their parents had no clue what to do about them. They didn't understand how 'normal' parents could have a child born with special powers. So once their powers manifested for the first time and their parents found out about them, their parents kicked them out into the streets. Luckily the school has ways of tracking new powers, so they send a teacher to find the children and bring them back to the school. Sadly, for some, the school is their only home now," Brayden adds.

"That sounds terrible. How could someone kick out their child because they are different from them? They do realize that their child is still a product of both of them, don't they?" Ian can't believe what he is hearing. "I feel sorry for those parents then. They choose to remove themselves from their own child and never get to see just how special their creation of life really is, or who they become. It really is those parents that end up losing the most in the end. Their offspring could become a leader, fighter, hero, or an inspiration to others. These parents are left out and in the dark. Until that one day when they see the child they gave away in the news or in an article about all the help and work they have done over the years. Then they have to feel the pain of knowing what they did was wrong," Ian expresses how he is feeling.

"You're right. You and I are lucky enough to have families that truly care about us and accept us for who we are," Brayden finishes, as Jax comes walking into the room.

"How was the security walk?" Ian asks.

"No signs of Mason or his men, yet. I'm still going to keep an eye out though," Jax replies. "So, what have you two been doing while I was gone?"

"Nothing really. Just talking about the school. But now that we are all here, we need to start working on a plan for when we arrive in San Antonio and in Houston. I'm sure we will have no issues in San Antonio, but I can guarantee we will in Houston," Brayden tells the both of them.

"I will agree with you about Houston. But I am not taking any chances in San Antonio just because you were told by someone, who took over your body, that we would be safe until then," Jax stipulates. "I think we need to sit down and start planning for both stations."

Brayden and Ian agree as Jax takes a seat at the table to join them. Then the planning begins.

***

Just as they are finishing up the small details of a complete escape plan and safe route to the school, in a quick flash, there stands Kenzie. Jax and Brayden are frozen, which must be the only way Kenzie can teleport, and Ian can tell something is wrong with her.

"Ian! I'm so glad to see you. I need your help to save my little brother. I don't have time to explain it all to you right now, but can you go through a mirror again? Except this time, I need you to go through the mirror in my brother's bedroom. Please! We need to hurry. His life is in danger," Kenzie finishes out of breath.

"Kenzie, what is going on? I don't know if I can do that again," Ian answers back.

"There is some man at my parents' house. A Mr. Mason, and he said he has been watching all of us. After he talked to me, I was sent back to the basement to be locked away again. But before the door shut completely, I heard Mr. Mason tell my father, 'Get me the boy!'" Kenzie exclaims. "I can't let them hurt him. He does not have powers like we do. If we hurry, we may be able to get to him first. Please, Ian! I'm begging you, for Connor's sake!"

Ian grabs Kenzie by the hand and leads her to the bathroom, which is the only place in the room on the sleeper car with a mirror. He is determined to do whatever he can to help Connor, for Kenzie. Once Kenzie and Ian are directly in front of the mirror, Ian just stands there not knowing what to do.

"What's wrong?" Kenzie inquires.

"To be honest, I have only done this once before, and that was the time I saw you. I don't really know how I did it then," Ian replies disappointedly.

"Now is not the time to be freezing up. That's my thing anyway. Listen, close your eyes. Now try to imagine Connor's room as I describe it to you, okay?" Kenzie insists. "Imagine a small boy's room. There is a single bed in the shape of a race car. Along the wall opposite of the bed, there is a three drawer dresser that has a mirror sitting on top of it. There is a window on your left. Do you see it?"

"Yes, it's starting to take shape. Keep going!" Ian instructs.

"Okay, good. Now, the walls are painted a light blue, like the sky on a clear day. Under the window is a multi-colored toy box over loaded with toys all around it. There is a little boy. He has brown hair, pale skin, in onesie pajamas that have race cars on them as well," Kenzie stops as she is looking at the image forming in the mirror.

"Now, open your eyes and reach into the mirror and grab Connor. *Now*!" Kenzie demands.

Just as Ian is opening his eyes, he also sees the place he has been guided to by Kenzie. Even though he is surprised it worked, he knows he has no time to spare.

Ian not only puts his hands and arms into the mirror, he also, using the sink for leverage, puts his head and upper body through the mirror. Ian knows he will need as much of his upper body strength as he has to grab Connor and pull him through the mirror. Ian's only fear is that he may scare the boy and will not be able to grab him. Just as Ian is coming through the mirror in to Connor's room, he notices Connor has his back turned towards him.

"Connor," Ian announces in somewhat of a loud whisper. "Hey, Connor. I'm a friend of Kenzie's."

Just as Connor turns around, Ian reassures him, "Now, don't be scared. I am here to take you to your sister."

As Connor finishes turning around, he looks at Ian with a very surprising look on his face. He does not look scared, but more excited. "How are you in my mirror?" Connor inquires.

"Well, it's a long story. Let's just say there are things I can do, with your sister's help, that other people can't do," Ian replies. "Now, do you want to come with me to see Kenzie?"

"Yes, where is she?" Connor asks.

"She is actually on the other side of this mirror. Come over here and I can bring you to her," Ian explains.

As Connor stands up and starts towards Ian and the mirror, his bedroom door springs open. It is Connor's fake father, Jerry. Jerry has been ordered to get Connor and bring him downstairs to speak with Mason. Jerry does not know what to think, as he first sees a boy hanging halfway out of the mirror. At first, he stands frozen in the door with his mouth open. Once he regains his composure, he rushes towards Connor.

"Connor, hurry. We don't have much time!" Ian exclaims, reaching out as far as he can. Just as he has ahold of Connor's hands, Jerry is making a jump for Connor. Ian pulls Connor towards him as fast as he can, wrapping his arms around Connor and pulling himself, with Connor, back through the mirror. Ian only has Connor halfway through the bathroom mirror when he suddenly stops making progress.

"Pull harder! Don't stop! Ian, pull my brother through the mirror!" Kenzie is yelling frantically.

"I'm trying! Come help me," Ian orders Kenzie. "It's like something is holding him back. Connor, why have you stopped? What's holding you?" Ian questions him.

"I think my father has ahold of my feet. I feel something holding them," Connor replies.

"Connor, listen to me. I need you to start kicking as hard as you can. Can you do that for me?" Kenzie is pleading with her little brother.

With that, Connor kicks his feet as hard as he can. Even though they cannot see his feet, Ian and Kenzie know he is trying his best.

Jerry is trying to keep a grip on Connor's feet. Still unsure of what is even happening, Jerry calls out for Delores to come help. All Jerry can see is a pair of short legs sticking out of the mirror.

While Jerry struggles to keep ahold of little, kicking feet, Delores comes rushing into the room. As she enters Connor's room, the shock of what she is witnessing causes her to let out a scream. Her scream causes Jerry to stumble and lose his grip on Connor's feet, and through the mirror they go.

Jerry gives Delores a look of terror and disappointment, as if saying to her, if not for her scream, he would not have lost the grip he had on Connor's little legs.

"Why in the world would you come into the room screaming?" Jerry demands to know of Delores. "Now, do you want to be the one who tells Mason we lost Connor?"

Before Delores can answer, Mason is walking into the room behind her.

"No need to tell me anything, as I can see with my own eyes your failure," Mason speaks with a tone that chills each of them to their core.

＊

Kenzie joins Ian at the bathroom mirror and takes ahold of one of Connor's arms. Kenzie is determined to make sure Connor is safe. Ian and Kenzie pull, while Connor keeps kicking.

"Don't stop kicking, Connor!" Kenzie is encouraging him. Just as Kenzie finishes saying his name, Connor comes flying all the way through the mirror. Ian and Kenzie, still pulling on Connor's arms, go flying backwards into the wall. Kenzie grabs Connor and pulls him as close to her as she can.

"*Okay*! Stop squeezing me. I. Can't. Breathe," Connor lets out in a muffled whisper.

"Sorry, I just can't believe you are here, and we did it," Kenzie replies to Connor while looking gratefully at Ian.

Ian is shaking his head as he pulls himself up off the bathroom floor with disbelief that he actually pulled Connor through the mirror. While Kenzie and Ian sit on the floor looking at each other, both with looks of accomplishment, they can hear Jax asking about them in the other room. Jax and Brayden have become unfrozen and notice Ian is missing.

Jax comes bursting into the bathroom. As he notices Ian is not alone, a shocked look comes across his face. "What in the world is going on in here?" Jax demands to know. "And just how did you two get here?" he asks, as he notices Kenzie and Connor sitting on the floor with Ian. "Who is he?" Jax asks, while pointing at Connor.

"Well, this is my little brother, Connor," Kenzie answers, "and the rest is a long story, which I will be glad to let Ian tell you." Kenzie is just happy her brother is in her arms and safe, for the time being.

Chapter 11

All Aboard?

There are five of them now heading to San Antonio for an eight and a half hour layover before they can board their last train to Houston. During this time, they are devising a plan together for the safety of them all. Just as the mysterious person who had taken over Brayden's body earlier on this train from Chicago to San Antonio had stated, 'they would see no trouble until they made it to Houston,' they have had no trouble.

Once they arrive in San Antonio, make it from the 21 Texas Eagle, and onto the Sunset Limited #2 for the last leg of their travels with no problems, Jax will then know they can trust what the mysterious person has told them.

Since they suspect they will encounter some action in Houston with Mason and his men, they have to be prepared. The train from San Antonio to Houston is only five hours, so they have little time to plan.

Jax, Brayden, and Ian do most of the planning for two reasons. One, they all three believe Kenzie needs to spend some time with her brother. She needs to explain a few things to him, because they are sure he is very confused by everything that has transpired over the last hour. The second reason is that Jax thinks Kenzie is too young to be able to help them, and he does not want to risk her getting hurt if she doesn't need to fight. So they agree to just leave her with Connor while they come up with different strategies.

Jax has a printout of the train station in Houston. They use this as their guide for coming up with the best exit plans. The Amtrak station in Houston is very small. Not only is it small, but they will have to exit the train outside of the station, out in the open. Once they are off of the train, they will have to make their way over to the only entry/exit to the actual station. Then after that, and if they make it inside, the only other entry/exit is across the entire station all the way on the other side of the small building. They know that they are going to have to depend on the cover of a group getting off the train in Houston if they are to make it out of the station safely. "There is only one problem with this part of the plan," Jax expresses to Brayden and Ian.

"And what is that?" Brayden asks.

"The train, the Sunset Limited #2, continues on from Houston to Louisiana. So even if the train is full, it does not mean there will be a large crowd getting off in Houston," explains Jax. "Now do you see how that can cause a problem for us? We have to account for every possible scenario."

"Can we take a break from planning for just a little bit?" Ian asks the other two. "I would like to take some time and not have to think about fighting or how to avoid a fight for a little while. I still don't know how to control my new powers or even my Time Keeper powers. Ever since my seventeenth birthday, my life has been non-stop, from becoming eighteen, then seventeen again, to having a best friend and losing her completely from my life, and not just my life, but history completely, and now this with Mason. I want to take some time to just forget about all of this and just remember how it was to be normal. Is that too much to ask?" Ian requests with sadness in his voice.

"Yeah, sure, Ian. Take all the time you need. Are you going to be okay?" Jax replies with concern.

"I don't know if I am okay, or even will be, right now. That's why I need time to myself," Ian lets them both know before walking over to his bunk bed.

***

"So, what all do you know about what is going on?" Kenzie asks Connor.

"What do you mean?"

"Aren't you at least somewhat freaked out after being pulled through a mirror?" Kenzie questions Connor.

"That was so cool! Do you think we can do it again?" Connor sounds excited.

"You weren't scared? I mean, there was an older boy sticking halfway through your dresser mirror calling you by name. Then he asks you to trust him and go to him, which you do, and he grabs you and starts pulling you through the mirror. And after all that, you weren't scared?" Kenzie is surprised.

"Not really. I've kind of gotten used to strange things happening around our home. Like that time you moved really fast, or the time I was frozen because I was grabbing for your doll and I was going to through it out the treehouse window. Then the next thing I know, the doll is in your hands and you are beside me. I didn't even see you move," Connor admits to Kenzie.

"You know about that?"

"Yes."

"How come you never said anything to me about it before?"

"I don't know. I didn't want to sound crazy, or anything," Connor comforts Kenzie with his answer.

"I guess you are right. That would have been a hard conversation for either of us to start," Kenzie replies with a laugh.

Next thing they know, they are both laughing. Kenzie can't remember the last time they were actually having fun and being happy together. She is so glad to be able to have this time with her brother now. These are the moments that will last a lifetime for her.

"Well, I hate to break up our fun, but there is something we do need to talk about. Are you okay with me telling you about some of it now?"

"Yeah. I know there are some things you have to tell me, so you might as well go ahead and get it over with. I would rather hear it from you now than later from someone else."

"I want you to know first, that we are safe, and no one can separate us again, okay?" Kenzie reassures Connor before continuing. "Let me start by telling you just how brave you are. There are not many kids that have been through what you have been through, even just today, and are still strong enough to talk about it. So thank you."

Connor gives Kenzie a look of love that only siblings can understand, and Kenzie knows he is ready to hear more.

"Well, you need to know that we cannot go back home again. Those people, the ones we know as Mom and Dad, are not our real parents. I'm not sure of all the details about them, but I promise they are not our real parents. But I know they want to do us harm. Do you understand?"

"Yes, I understand, sort of. I mean, what are we going do for a home now? Who is going to take care of us?"

Kenzie has to take a few minutes to think about how to answer that question, considering she has not thought that far ahead. *What are we going to do?* Kenzie thinks to herself.

About what? It's Ian replying to her thought.

How are you listening to my thoughts now?

I'm not. You are in my head. But since you are here, what are you worried about?

Well, Connor just asked me who was going to take care of us now that we don't have a home to go to, or parents for that matter.

What are you talking about? Remember, you still owe me some explanation as to why we kidnapped your little brother in the first place.

Kenzie breaks off her thoughts with Ian as she is interrupted.

"Are you there?" Connor asks Kenzie.

"Yes, I'm here. Sorry, I just have not had time to think that far ahead. When I left the house this last time, and I heard Mr. Mason tell dad, I mean Jerry, to *'Get me the boy,'* I panicked and ended up here with Ian and the others. I'm not sure how my powers work, which I will explain more about them to you later. Since I was here with Ian, I asked him to reach through the mirror to get you to make sure you would be safe. That is as far as I have thought," Kenzie answers Connor.

"It's time to gather up all of our belongings. We are about to arrive at the San Antonio train station. Even though we have been told that we will not be harmed until we reach Houston, we still need to be alert. Now, we will arrive in San

Antonio at almost 10:00 p.m., which will work in our favor. I think we will have a better chance of walking in a group at night, which may make it harder for anyone to identify us, if anyone is watching," Jax informs the team. Everyone is moving around the small sleeper car gathering their things, everyone that is except Kenzie and Connor. They have everything the need, each other.

"Our next train does not leave until 6:25 a.m., so we have about eight and a half hours before we leave. I had thought of staying at a hotel down at the Riverwalk since it is usually packed with tourist.

The San Antonio Riverwalk is one story below the streets of the city. It's lined with plenty of places to eat and shop, along with a river running through it. It draws many tourists also because of the fact it is a connecting path to many places other than food and shopping. It is connected to places like the city's five Spanish Colonial Missions, which are now named a World Heritage Site, which includes the Alamo. During the spring, they host the annual Fiesta San Antonio that has a river parade featuring flowery boats that float down the river. Now that's a sight to see," Jax gives the history lesson with such passion. You can tell just how much Jax loves history.

"Being that it is so late, most of the shops will be closed, so the streets will not be as crowded as I would prefer. So, I've decided we will take refuge in a 2-8-2 Baldwin Steam Locomotive, referred to as 'Mikado,' that is here at this station. Now this 2-8-2 was retired in 1956 and placed for display at Maverick Park which is near the station.

The 2-8-2 Steam Locomotives were named so as they represented their wheel arrangements of two leading wheels on one axle on the leading car, eight powered and coupled driving wheels on four axles, and two trailing wheels on one axle on the last car. In the early 1900's, the 2-8-2 Steam Engines replaced the 2-8-0 Consolidations as the main heavy freight train types. They were mostly used to haul lumber. During the summer, they would add a passenger car on the end to provide rides for locals and tourists, going only seven miles in East Texas, which only cost fifty cents at the time. One of the last remaining 2-8-2 engines is here at this train station. It was relocated here from the park in 2017," Jax finishes his history lesson.

The group has their things gathered and are standing still, listening to every word of Jax's story. *How does he know so much stuff?* Ian thinks to himself.

Good question. But don't you think he can hold back on the stories for now, until we are safe? Kenzie answers in Ian's mind.

Really? Can't I just have one thought to myself without getting an answer back?

Sorry. Like I said before, I can't control these powers.

I know. I'm sorry I snapped at you. I'll get Jax back on track, Ian assures Kenzie, before turning his attention to Jax.

"Shouldn't we be getting off this train, or do you have more stories to tell us first?" Ian asks Jax.

"Okay. Now I want you all to stay close to each other as we walk down the hall to the exit. Once we are off the train, do not follow the crowd. We are going to go to the front of this train and cross over the tracks to the other side. We need to get behind this train to get to the Mikado. Does everyone understand?" Jax asks his travel companions.

With quick nods of their heads, Jax turns and opens the sleeper cabin door, leading them out into the corridor of the car. They all exit one by one, close together as instructed, and follow Jax down the hall to the closest exit. They exit the train the same way they exited the cabin, one after another and close to each other.

Once they are all on the station platform, Jax turns right, walking them into the oncoming foot traffic of the other passengers leaving the train.

As they make their way to the front of the train they just rode from Chicago, Jax makes sure they are not being following. Once they are at the front of the train, after a quick look around, Jax ushers them hurriedly across the tracks in front of the lead car. Now that they are on the backside of the 21 Texas Eagle, they run down the tracks until they reach their destination, the 2-8-2 Mikado Steam Train. As luck would have it, there is a passenger car attached to it. All they have to do now is find a way onto the car.

"Now what?" Brayden asks Jax. "How are we supposed to get on this museum train that is locked up tight?"

"Do you ever listen to anything I tell you? I told you the story about how trains do not actually touch the ground, allowing for some magic to be used undetected. In other words, there is a way in for us. We just need to locate it, quickly," Jax snaps back.

"What should we be looking for, or do you not need us to help locate the entrance?" Ian inquires.

"All I need right now is for you all to stay put, right here. I'll be right back," Jax replies.

Jax takes off around the corner of the Mikado, and out of sight of the group. A minute later, they hear Jax. "Okay, everyone. Over here. This is the way in."

Brayden turns to the other three, signaling them to follow him as he leads them around the corner of the 2-8-2 towards Jax's location.

"This right here is a portal we can go through to get onto the passenger car. Now, one thing you all need to know is that we can only go through one at a time, and we will not all come out in the same place on the train," Jax fills them in as he points at the portal.

"What do you mean? Where will we go? How will we find each other?" Kenzie is freaking out, worrying about Connor.

"Don't worry, Kenzie. We will all be on this train car, just in different rooms. Once you are through the portal and on the car, make your way to room 303 and wait in the hall. Can you all remember those instructions?" Jax asks, while looking at Connor.

"Room 303," Connor replies, looking bravely at Kenzie.

"Then you will go first, Connor. Kenzie you will go after him, understood?"

"Yes, I understand. Connor, if you get lost, just yell my name, because I'll be right behind you through the portal," Kenzie finishes as she is hugging Connor.

After their hug is over, Connor turns and walks through the portal, disappearing into the void. Next, Kenzie goes through, then Ian, and then Brayden.

As Brayden is going through the portal, he hears some guards yelling at Jax. They have seen him. Before he can turn around and go back out of the portal, he is already aboard the train in a room. Knowing it is out of his control, all he can think is, *I hope we are all aboard.*

Chapter 12

Where is Everyone?

Connor walks through the portal onto the 2-8-2 Mikado Steam Train passenger car only a few seconds before he is in a room on the train. He turns around as quickly as he can to see if the passageway is still open. But to his surprise, he only sees his own reflection from the room window. He does not expect the portal to close so fast.

"Room 303," Connor reminds himself out loud. "I have to get to room 303."

Connor takes a moment to make sure no one else is coming through the magical entrance into his room, or if Jax was right, and they all will end up in different rooms. *Guess Jax was telling the truth. No one is coming in here except me!* Connor thinks to himself as he is making his way to the room door.

Now that he is at the door, he is a little scared. He is the first one through the portal and does not know how long it may be before Kenzie comes through, plus he just entered a locked train through a magical portal. He has every reason to be a little frightened, but he pushes his fears down and places his hand on the door latch. Connor pulls the lever and tries to slide the pocket door open, but it does not move. It's not locked, but it feels stuck.

Now Connor begins to panic. He feels like he is stuck in a room on the train. "How can I get to room 303 if I am stuck in this room? How is Kenzie going to be able to find me?" Connor is thinking out loud again.

"Kenzie!" Connor yells, but gets no reply. "Kenzie," he tries again, while falling to sit on the floor in front of the door.

***

Kenzie rushes into the portal, ending up in her room, where she wastes no time to look around. Kenzie knows the portal is closed, and she is alone in the room just as Jax had explained to her. She takes long strides over to the door of the room, so she can head out to look for Connor and room 303.

Reaching the door, Kenzie is caught off guard when she grabs the door lever. Upon trying to open the door, she finds it doesn't move. The door is stuck. *How is this possible? Why wouldn't Jax tell us about this?*

Instead of waiting for answers, Kenzie decides to try and use her powers to teleport to Connor. She has not actually figured out how to access her powers, or control them, but she has to try something. There is a drawback to her using her powers though, and she knows it. *What if I teleport myself back home, or who knows where? How will that be any help to Connor, or myself, at this moment?*

I can't take that risk, not right now. I have to learn how to control my powers before I create any more, Kenzie talks herself out of using them. She is going to have to find another way.

***

As Ian is making his way through his entry into his room, he stumbles over an old suitcase that is sitting on the floor. Ian does not have time to gain control over his unbalanced body upon entering his room, and hits the floor, landing on his left arm. In an instant, pain shoots through his body, especially from his left hand.

Ian looks at the suitcase sitting on his room floor and gives it a swift kick. Next thing he knows, the suitcase is gone. He manages to kick it into the portal before it is completely closed.

"Oops," Ian laughs out loud, which only increases his pain. The pain lasts for a few minutes, then Ian is back to himself. Now that the pain is gone, along with the luggage, Ian reaches out to touch the wall. Just as he suspected, the portal is closed.

Well that was funny, but enough playing around. I have to get out of here and find room 303, along with the others, Ian tells himself. Getting up off the floor takes him a moment, as the pain maybe gone, but his left arm is still a bit stiff.

Once Ian is up, he starts moving towards the door to the room where he ended up. He grabs the door handle and gives it a pull, but he faces the same issues as Kenzie and Connor. The door in his room is stuck as well.

As much as Ian has been through in the past few weeks, he does not panic. Instead he begins to look for a mirror. *Might as well give my new powers some practice.* Sadly enough to Ian, after a look around his room, there are no mirrors. *Well, this is not an option. I need some reflective surface in order to use my gift!*

***

Brayden is now on his way through the portal. But before he can exit into his room, he swears he can see some kind of luggage fly past him. Unable to turn himself back around, after looking at the UFL (unidentified flying luggage), he is entering his room backwards. With some quick thinking and plenty of training, he is prepared.

As Brayden hits the floor, he rolls over backwards until his feet are on the ground, leaving him in a grounded attack position. He knows nothing is coming after him, and he's alone in his room, but it is the best landing position he could come up with within the split second after he entered the portal.

Taking a deep breath and standing up from his crouching attack stance, Brayden can't help but think of Jax. The last thing he heard was someone, a security guard he hopes, yelling at Jax to stop.

Now is not the time to worry about Jax. I need to get out of here, find room 303 and make sure the others are okay.

He makes his move over to the door of his room, but finds himself with a stuck door, just like the others.

***

Jax watches Brayden vanish through the portal, then looks to see who is yelling at him. He hopes whoever it is did not see anyone go through the portal. He is prepared to handle whoever is coming, as long as they don't know about the others.

Before Jax can turn completely around, he feels a hand on his shoulder. As Jax is in the process of turning around to see who has ahold of him, an old suitcase shoots past him.

Jax does not know what to think, but the flying luggage makes connection with the security guard who has already caught up to Jax. The flying suitcase connects so hard with the security guard that he is laid out cold on the ground. Jax bends down to check his pulse and breathing, and both are fine.

Now that the guard is knocked out and no one else is around, Jax makes a quick jump into the portal. Jax does not know where the suitcase came from, but he takes his precautions while in the portal. Without any new flying objects passing him, he lands firmly in his room.

Jax has no time to waste, as he is sure the others are a bit scared right now. There is one thing he didn't tell them, but it was to keep them calm and to make sure they went through the portal. Jax makes his way to the door to his room, pulls the lever and ...

***

Connor, Kenzie, Ian, and Brayden are all pulling on their respective room door levers at the same time, when all of a sudden the doors all fly open. Everyone is falling out of their own rooms at the exact same time.

***

The door to Jax's room opens up with no issues. He steps out into the hallway from his room, while at the same time, everyone else is falling out of the exact same room. As they all collide with each other, they end up in a dog pile in the hall, with Brayden on the bottom.

While they are all grunting and groaning as they un-pile, Jax is standing next to them laughing. "By the way, there is something I didn't mention to any of you. I'm sorry I had to leave something out about your rooms, but it was for the best," Jax explains.

Not one of the others even asks Jax what he left out, because they all came to the same conclusion. They all assumed that he left out the fact that their room doors would remain unable to open until they were all on the train. Little do they know that is only part of it, there is another part Jax held back.

"Don't you want to know what I left out?" Jax asks the group.

"I think we have already figured it out. We were all stuck in our rooms until we were all on the train," Ian answers.

"Well, you are only halfway to the full truth. If you all don't mind, would you please all look right up here for me?" Jax asks as he is pointing at the room number they are laying in front of. "Now do you understand?"

They all just sat there on the floor, staring at the room number they all just fell out of, Room 303.

"Are you joking? How were we all in the same room at the same time, but also alone?" Kenzie is asking the questions now.

"Well, remember when I said you had to enter the portal one at a time? Well, that is just it. You were all in the room at different times, but the same room nonetheless. And yes, once I made it onto the train, I was able to open the door causing all the different times to come together. I didn't tell you about this part because I didn't want anyone to worry," Jax explains in detail.

"By different times, what kind of time are you talking about?" asks Ian, as his powers have more to do with actual time.

"We will talk more about that once we are back in the room," Jax replies.

"You want us to go back into the room we just got out of?" Connor is asking the question this time.

"Yes, but it will be okay now. Now that we are all together, we are able to go in and be in the same time," Jax reassures Connor as he is opening the door to Room 303.

Everyone is standing behind Jax as he opens the door, not sure what to expect once the door is open. But nothing happens, the door opens with ease and Jax leads them back into room 303.

***

The hours have passed by while they occupy the room. Connor and Kenzie took this time to get some rest. The other three stayed up talking.

"It was the strangest thing. Next thing I knew, there was an old suitcase flying through the air hitting the security guard and knocking him out cold," Jax tells Ian and Brayden with a laugh.

"I knew I saw some type of luggage flying past me in the portal right before I landed in here," Brayden laughs as well. "Where did it come from?"

"That would be my fault," confesses Ian. "When I ended up in this room during my time, there was an old suitcase sitting right in front of the portal entrance. I tripped over it as I entered the room, causing me to land on my arm. Because of my pain, I kicked the suitcase, but I didn't know it would go out through the portal."

"I'm glad you did kick it, because you kicked it just in time too. If not for you kicking that suitcase, I may have not made it on the train. So thank you," Jax thanks Ian.

"No problem," Ian replies as they are all laughing.

"I think we all need to get some rest like Connor and Kenzie. Tomorrow is going to be a long day," Jax tells the two boys. And just like that, they head to their spots in the room and lay down. It doesn't take long for either of them to pass out fast asleep.

***

It's 5:00 a.m. and Jax is waking up the troops.

"It's time to get up everyone. We need to get off this train and onto our next one without any complications," Jax is instructing them.

"What time is it?" Connor asks while trying to rub the sleep from his eyes.

"Early enough for us to get a move on and get off this train without being seen. Good news though, the exit portal is at the front of this train. If the guards are looking in the area I was last seen, they will be in the wrong spot. So get up, get your things, and let's get a move on. Our next train leaves for Houston at 6:25 a.m.," Jax informs them.

Everyone does as Jax has asked. They are all up, things gathered, and now standing at the door waiting for Jax to open it.

Jax gives the door lever a tug and it slides open, letting them out of the room and into the hallway. They all exit Room 303 and follow Jax to the front of the train, making their way towards the exit portal.

The group makes their way safely from the 2-8-2 Mikado to the Sunset Limited #2. This is the train that will head to Houston. This train ride is only four hours and forty-five minutes, so boarding the train early gives them time to settle in before they get back to safety strategies and also how they ended up with Connor and Kenzie.

Chapter 13

Getting out of the Station

The train sways with a steady motion, as it runs down the tracks, moving them closer and closer towards their final destination, Houston.

While Ian finishes filling Jax and Brayden in on his new found gift of being able to not only see people and places in mirrors, but he can also pull people through them, Kenzie keeps ahold of Connor tightly. Kenzie is so happy that she and Connor are safe, but she is unsure of what will happen next.

Now that everyone is all caught up on the current events that have transpired with Kenzie and Connor, they all take the next few hours to get some rest. They know they will need their strength once they arrive in Houston. They know Mason will be waiting for them there, and he will be even more determined to capture them now that Kenzie and Connor are out of his reach.

***

"Why didn't you tell me that Ian can go through mirrors and take people back through them with him?" Mason asks Kayla.

"He did what?" Kayla sounds surprised. "How am I supposed to know he can do that?"

"You were his best friend for seventeen years," replies Mason.

"Yes, before I removed myself from his past. Maybe this is a gift that is a result of me removing myself from his history. Did you ever think of that?" Kayla sounds pleased with her answer.

"There better not be any more surprises, for your sake," Mason threatens Kayla, as he raises his hand back, but does not strike her.

***

With thirty minutes left before the train reaches Houston, Ian gathers his belongings. Ian is not as scared as he was when he first boarded the train to Houston, now that Kenzie and

Connor have joined them. Ian feels they have strength in numbers, and they are now a group of five.

Everyone seems to have higher spirits now that they are all together. Connor seems to be adjusting to his newly found friends and surroundings after having been pulled through a mirror. Kenzie is enjoying having her little brother with her. This way she doesn't have to worry about him as much. Brayden and Jax are enjoying stories of Chicago and the school. Ian is just sitting back on his bed, taking in all the conversations and the reactions of everyone.

As the time passes, the train begins to slow down. The train is pulling up to their last stop, the Houston Train Station. Now is the time for them to be ready and on guard. They know Mason will try everything he can to stop them, once they reach Houston. So far, everything the mysterious person, who had taken control of Ian and Brayden, had told them has been true.

Jax is already looking out of the room's window, as the train begins to slow to a stop. Jax looks for any sign of Mason or his men. He tells everyone to stay in the room until he returns. Jax explains to the group that he wants to check out their possible exits off the train. Jax walks out of the room, closes and locks the door, before continuing. Jax makes his way up and down the corridor, glancing out of each window as he passes them, surveying the station's platform. Jax knows Mason will be careful not to reveal his presence, but Jax thinks at least one of his followers will slip up. So far Jax can see nothing out of the ordinary. He witnesses busy travelers getting on and off the train.

Jax makes his way back to the room where Ian and the others are waiting, knowing it is now or never. They have little time to get off the train before it starts onto its next destination.

"Okay, everyone, listen up," Jax orders his companions as he unlocks the door and enters the room. "We are not going to have much time to get from here to the school. The school is one and a half miles from here. So we will need to be walking at a fast pace," Jax instructs the group.

"Why are we walking instead of taking a taxi, or a bus?" Ian asks.

"If we are on foot, we will be able to keep an eye on each other as well as our surroundings. If we rode in a taxi, or a bus, we would be confined to that space. That could put innocent people in danger. Besides, any one of Mason's followers could be driving the taxi, or the bus," Jax replies.

"Okay, now I need everyone to gather their things and follow me," Jax commands.

The group does as they are told and, with their bags on their backs except for Kenzie who has Connor, follows Jax out of the cabin door. Everyone is feeling a little rush of excitement as they enter the hallway of the train and make their way to the exit.

Everything on the train platform looks normal. Busy passengers are making their way on and off the train, just as Jax had witnessed while he was checking things out earlier. Some people are waving goodbye, while others are greeting their friends or loved ones with great joy and hugs. Ian can't help but to think how different people are in Texas than in Brooklyn. In Brooklyn, people try to avoid even making eye contact with others as they move around the city, much-less screams of joy and emotions. Ian knows it will take some getting used to, but he is excited.

The group exits the train, following Jax as instructed, onto the train station platform. Jax leads them through a group of travelers so as to blend in on their way to the station exit. While they walk with the crowd, Ian is looking around taking in the décor of the station. Ian notices it is nothing like Union Station. Houston Train Station is much older and obviously has not been as well cared for over the years.

Everything is going as planned so far. The group of five have made their way through the station, blending in from crowd to crowd, getting closer and closer to the station exit. Jax knows that getting out of the train station will not be the hardest part, but to him, even a small victory is still a victory.

The feeling of the small victory is not long lived, because blocking their exit is Mason. Mason is standing not only between them and the exit to Houston's main streets, but the crowd in the station spreads out around them, encompassing them. This is not something they had expected.

Jax had figured they would encounter Mason and his followers at some point before making it to the school, but he did not expect Mason to have this large of a following with him. After noticing Mason, Jax takes a quick survey of Ian, Kenzie, Connor and Brayden, before searching his surroundings for a way out. His group is all together and accounted for and looks ready for anything.

"What are we going to do, Jax?" Ian whispers.

"Give me a minute. I just need a moment to think," Jax whispers back to Ian.

Before Jax can finish with his thoughts, Kenzie speaks to Ian telepathically, *I can try and freeze time, like I did before.*

No. It's too risky. Remember, both times you froze time before, you were teleporting, and you and I were the only two that did not freeze, Ian thinks back to Kenzie.

Just as Ian finishes his reply to Kenzie, Jax speaks. "Everyone stay calm, and don't make any rash decisions. We need to keep our heads about us," Jax tells his group as if he knows what Kenzie is thinking.

After a few minutes of silence, Mason finally speaks. "Jax, it's been a long time. I have been waiting for this day. The day you and I would see each other again," Mason finishes with a glance over to Ian.

"And just how do you think this meeting will go?" Jax questions Mason.

"Let's just say I know a lot more than you do. I know all of your new friends' names, and about their gifts. We are prepared for them all, if they are used," Mason says to the group looking all too pleased with himself.

How does he know so much about us? Ian wonders to himself.

I'm sorry, Ian. This is all my fault. I had no choice. Mason said if I didn't help him, he would destroy my bloodline, the mysterious person is responding once again to Ian's thoughts.

Who are you? How do you know me? Why are you helping us? Ian questions the mystery voice.

There is no time to explain everything now. There is one thing Mason has not prepared for. Since he recently just found out about your gift to create passageways in reflective surfaces, he is not prepared for you to use it, replies the voice.

Well, that's not going to help us at this moment, as there are no mirrors here for me to use. And I'm not even sure if, or how, I can get all of us through a mirror anyway. Any other suggestions? Ian replies in a more aggressive tone than he intended to use.

Ian, think. Are mirrors the only things that show reflections? I have to leave you for now, before he realizes I've been speaking to you. You only have a small amount of time if you are going to do this, so start thinking, the voice finishes as Ian feels her leave his mind.

Mason and Jax are in a discussion about how they are just children, or something like that, while Ian quickly looks around the station. Ian is looking for anything that will cast a reflection that is also large enough for them all to go through. That's when Ian finds what he is looking for. It is perfect. But where is Ian going to take them? Ian has to think fast.

Kenzie, are you there? Ian thinks, hoping she is in his mind.

Yes, Ian, I'm here. What's the plan? Kenzie replies back.

I have an idea that I think will work. Don't worry, everything is going to be fine. I need you to stall Mason for three minutes and to keep his focus on you and Connor. Try and let the others know what's going on somehow. When I give the signal, you all will need to follow me, to there, Ian says to Kenzie, while looking to his right.

Kenzie follows Ian's gaze, and then she understands. *Got it,* she replies back to Ian.

While Kenzie quickly whispers to Brayden and Jax, Ian closes his eyes.

***

Ian is thinking back to when they were on the train and Brayden and Jax were talking about the school. Suddenly, Ian is standing in the train car listening to their stories again. Somehow, he must have stored that moment in the Time Keeper, and now he is accessing it. Ian does not know how he put that memory in the Time Keeper, but now is not the time to figure that out. He is just glad it is there.

Ian turns his attention to the two of them talking about the school. What wasn't interesting to Ian the first time, is now the most important conversation of his life. Since Ian has never been to the school, he needs to know as much as possible about the school if he is going to be able to get them out of the train station safely.

Jax and Braden are reminiscing about some previous school events, a dance, and some academic competitions. None of this Ian can find useful. He knows he does not have much time, or at least he does not actually know what happens during current time while he is accessing a memory in the Time Keeper. To be on the safe side, Ian assumes he needs to be quick.

Since Ian has accessed his own memory, he is actually in his own body. Not wanting to change the future, but also assuming time is against him, he makes the decision to join the conversation this time around. He understands the consequences of what can possibly happen if he reveals too much information in his memory, so he only asks his own questions about the school. This way he can try to minimize changing the future.

"Wow, the school sounds like it has a lot of different activities there. Do they have any sports teams? I mean, is this the only school in the world, or are there other schools out there they can compete with?" Ian questions.

"Well, there are a few other schools, but not in North America. There are several schools across the world on other continents to help find, house, and train new gifted students near them. So, we don't really have sports teams, but we do compete in events. Some events we break up into groups to compete groups against each other. Other times we are all competing against each other individually, each student for themselves," Jax replies to Ian.

"That's cool. Well, what are the sleeping quarters like? Do they have big mirrors in them? You know me, Jax, I like to make sure I look my best before leaving for the day," Ian directs question.

"To be honest, Ian, there really are no mirrors in the school. Mirrors can be used for so many different things in our world. So to reduce anything from happening with the use of them, we removed them all. We do, however, give each student their own personal mirror they can use for getting ready each morning. You will learn all about the dangers of mirrors at the school. But don't worry, I'm sure Brayden can let you know if your bow tie is crooked," Jax cracks a joke at Ian.

They have to have something in that school with a reflective surface. Think, Ian!

"Water!" Ian shouts out loud by accident.

"What about water? Are you thirsty, or are you just needing a bath?" this time it is Brayden snapping back with the jokes.

"No, sorry for yelling. I was just thinking about how much I am going to miss swimming, unless the school has a pool?" inquires Ian.

"Of course we have a pool. What kind of school do you think we are going to?" again it's Brayden with the jokes. "We have the most amazing heated, saltwater, rooftop pool in the city. Don't worry, you will enjoy swimming even more than you do now!"

"Yes!" exclaims Ian. "Okay, you can go back to your regular conversation now," Ian insists.

Jax and Brayden look at each other, and Ian is quiet again.

***

Ian finishes with the memory. When he opens his eyes, he is back at the station exit with the others, exactly at the time he had left. Kenzie seems to be doing a great job of keeping Mason's attention on her.

Before Mason knows what is going on, Ian grabs Kenzie's wrist and is yelling, "NOW!"

Kenzie holds on to Connor, as Ian drags them behind him, with Brayden and Jax following along close behind. Ian's group seems to be catching on to the plan before Mason can. As Mason screams for his followers to stop them, Kenzie and Connor have already jumped into a fountain in the center of the station, followed by Jax and Brayden, all of whom disappear through the watery surface. Just after Ian jumps towards the fountain, hoping it will work, he catches a glimpse of a young girl. She is standing behind Mason. As Ian is falling into the fountain, he knows who she is. But it is too late. He is already going under the surface of the water.

As Ian emerges from the rooftop pool at the school, he is shouting her name, "KAYLA!" Just before he passes out at the feet of his friends.

Chapter 14

Until Next Time

As Ian is making his way through the fountain to the rooftop pool at the school, he is screaming Kayla's name. Jax quickly reaches down to grab Ian by his arm before he goes back under the water. Jax catches his arm just in time, because Ian has passed out from the strain of using too much of his powers so fast.

Jax pulls Ian over to the side of the pool where the others are standing. They pull him out of the water and lay him on the ground on his back. Jax bends over Ian and checks his breathing and pulse which are both fine, confirming to Jax that Ian has just passed out. Jax orders the others to help him carry Ian down to the infirmary. That is the hospital area of the school where Ian can stay in until he regains consciousness.

With guidance from Jax, Brayden takes Ian by his legs while Jax has him by his shoulders. Kenzie and Connor take charge of running over to the glass doors that lead into the rooftop lounge of the school. With Kenzie pulling and holding the door open, Connor runs into the lounge to get help. To Connor's surprise, the lounge is empty. *Where is everybody?* Connor turns and runs back to his sister, who is still holding the doors open, as Jax and Brayden are making their way through with Ian.

"Jax, what do you want me to do? I thought there would be people in that room over there. But it's empty," Connor sounds defeated.

"The elevators are right down that hallway," Jax replies while pointing to the hall on his left. "Go down that hall and push the button to call for the elevator. If the elevator opens before we get there, press the button that looks like two doors staying open, or just stand in front of the door, and don't let it close."

Without a word, Connor takes off running down the hall Jax is pointing towards, until he reaches the elevators. Connor has never used, nor seen, an elevator before. He is standing in front of three metal doors. The three doors are closed and there is one button in the center of them. The button says "Down" on it, so Connor pushes it. Just as Connor removes his finger from the button, the doors to the far left open.

Connor assumes that since those doors are opening, they must be doors to an elevator. He runs over to it to try to keep the doors open as Jax had instructed. Once he is at the open doors, he steps into a small room with picture scenes of gardens and forest animals on the walls. He takes one look at the panel on the wall by the door and notices all the different buttons on it. That is when panic starts to rise up inside him.

Connor is looking at all of these different buttons on the panel. To him, none of the buttons look like doors opening. He sees some with numbers on them, some with bells, and still others have funny shaped arrows on them. Before Connor can make any decisions about the buttons, the door begins to close. That is when the panic is gone, and his instincts take over. Connor does not have time to think. He quickly sticks his arm through the remaining crack between the closing door and the wall of the elevator. This action causes the door to open up again. This is when Connor understands what Jax meant by putting his body in front of the door. Now that he knows what to do, he takes his stance between the door and the wall. He holds the door open with his body, waiting until they arrive with Ian, which is only a few seconds later.

Once they are all inside the elevator, Jax asks Connor to press the button that has the *I* with a circle around it. "That is the floor with the infirmary on it," Jax explains the symbol.

Connor reaches up and presses the button as instructed. And just like that, the doors close and the room they are in starts to move. Now since this is Connor's first time in a moving elevator, it is all fascinating to him, even though he is worried about Ian.

"What's wrong with him?" Kenzie asks Jax.

"I'm not sure. But I can promise you this, he will be okay. Try not to worry too much about Ian, and remember you have Connor who needs you now more than ever," Jax reassures Kenzie.

"You're right. I need to focus on Connor right now," Kenzie replies to Jax. "Hey, Connor? How are you doing right now? How is your first elevator ride?"

"Well, it feels different than going through a mirror or water, but it's not bad," Connor confesses. "I don't really understand what all the buttons are for, or how we are moving, or even what an elevator actually is, but I'm having fun."

Saving History – School Bound

This is when Jax chimes in with another history story.

"Well, let me give you a quick lesson while we have a moment. Maybe that is what we need to calm everyone down a little bit," Jax clarifies, before he starts with the history lesson.

"Let me start out by saying there are mixed stories about when the first elevator was created. Some say the elevator was used by the Romans in 336 B.C. Others say the elevator was first used by King Louis XV in 1743, for some personal private reasons let's say and leave it at that. Then there are the two British architects, Burton and Horner in 1823, who used elevators. But nowadays, we have come to know Elisha Otis to be associated with the elevator.

"Elisha Otis is the creator of the safety brake for elevators. If the rope was broken, or snapped, due to wear and tear, the brake would snap out and hit the walls of the elevator shaft, causing the elevator to stop falling. At the World's Fair of 1854 held at the Crystal Palace in New York, Otis demonstrated the safety brake by placing himself in an elevator for the viewers to watch. After he was up at the top in the elevator, he had the ropes cut with an ax. Everyone thought for sure he would fall to his death. But his safety brakes snapped out and stopped the elevator from falling for all to see. One person responsible for getting everyone hyped up about this stunt was Phineas Barnum. Now, even though Otis showed that his safety brake worked in 1854, the first public elevator was not installed until 1857 inside of a New York building," Jax finishes just as the elevator stops on their floor and the door opens.

"For those of you who maybe too young to remember when a circus was a big thing, Phineas Taylor Barnum was the world's first Showman. P. T. Barnum did not start out with just the circus, but he had other endeavors before then. When P. T. was twenty-two years old, he was successfully able to convince people that Joice Heth, a shriveled black woman, was a 161-year old nurse to General George Washington. It wasn't until her death when his human relic was exposed as a fake.

After a taste of being able to mislead people, P. T. continued to move forward to become the Greatest Showman. Not only did he purchase a five story museum full of waxed and stuffed animals, he went on to find real people that others found strange. To him, they were people that others were just curious about, so he created a show based on those curiosities. He found a set of Siamese twins, connected at their breastbones, as one of his first live curious acts. Then it was when he found a 25 inch tall man, Charles Stratton, who became known as General Tom Thumb, when P. T. sold 20 million tickets to the museum. This alone had him received by President Abraham Lincoln, and later commanded a performance before Queen Victoria.

P. T. Barnum was over 60 years old when he partnered with James A. Bailey to introduce the world to the 'Barnum and Bailey Circus.' Together they gave America a gigantic, memorable, popular place, with attractions in an attempt to be called 'The Greatest Show on Earth.' When P. T. was 81 years old, he fell very ill and asked that his obituary be printed before his death, so he may enjoy it. It was two weeks after the New York newspapers printed his obituary when P. T. Barnum died," Jax finishes his history of one of his favorite people.

Once the door is fully open, Connor shoots out of the elevator like a rocket yelling for help. By the time Brayden and Jax make it out with Ian, there are three orderlies standing in the hallway with a gurney for Ian.

"Good job, Connor," Jax boasts.

The orderlies take Ian and lay him down on the gurney. Jax, Brayden, Kenzie, and Connor are all standing in the hallway watching as Ian is being taken away by the orderlies. The orderlies are met by a doctor at the double doors at the end of the hall.

"Don't worry. We will take good care of him. We will let you know as soon as he is stable and ready for visitors," the doctor comforts the group. "Now, you four need to go and get some rest. We will call you as soon as we know something. I promise."

***

During Ian's time in the infirmary, Jax is able to get Brayden access to Ian.

Jax explains how Brayden's gift of dream watching can help them learn more information about a person that may, or may not, exist. He also explains that while Ian is still asleep, now is the perfect time to gather as much information as possible without hurting him.

The nurse agrees to Jax's request and allows Brayden access to Ian's room, and mind, as long as there are no signs of Ian being in any danger.

Ian is asleep for three days while Brayden uses his gift of dream watching to go into Ian's dreams and see what Ian is dreaming. Jax figures that while Ian is asleep, he will be dreaming of Kayla, since he was screaming her name when he made it through the passageway. The massive passageway was the one he created in the fountain at the Houston train station, which landed them at the school rooftop swimming pool, before Ian passed out.

Brayden uses these three days, not only to watch Ian's dreams, but to gather as much information as he can about Kayla. Brayden is lucky because Ian dreams a lot about Kayla. Brayden has a strange feeling while in Ian's dreams, a feeling like Ian's memories of Kayla are not real, but are real simultaneously.

Brayden has not only been watching Ian's dreams, but his memories as well. To Brayden's surprise, Ian's dreams are far from how the world actually is in comparison to his memories. Ian dreams of a world where everyone is accepted for being who they are, powers or not, while his memories are more of being bullied in school for him being different. He was bullied for being smart, yet not gloating about it, dressing nice, but not going over the top, basically just for being different. Brayden learns that Ian had it hard before finding out about his connection to the Time Keeper, like he was a target at school for no reason. Brayden could feel Ian's pain, and at the same time feel his happiness for being himself instead of pretending to be anyone else. Brayden couldn't help but feel ashamed of himself, because he had been a bully in school. Now, being able to see what an impact bullies made in Ian's life, Brayden begins to wonder about the lives he may have affected.

Brayden pushes his own thoughts to the side, for now anyway. He knows he will need to revisit them at another time, because he now knows his actions are inexcusable and may have consequences in the future. He turns his attention back to Ian.

Ian's dreams and memories also include his parents, their apartment, and even Belvedere Castle, which all feel genuine to Brayden. Then when Ian has any thoughts of Kayla, Brayden feels different. He feels empty. He can sense the strong feelings Ian has towards Kayla and the memories of her, except he can't see those memories.

Brayden has a hard time explaining this to Jax and Kenzie. The best way he can explain it is, "It's like watching a movie, then you have a scene that is removed, but the film is still there, running with no picture. I can see his thoughts of Kayla, but they feel like an empty blank spot in his mind.

I can tell you that she is very much real." He can tell the difference from one of Ian's memories and one of Ian's dreams, but when he thinks of Kayla, Brayden feels as if they are both a dream and a memory. Jax deduces it is because Kayla is real to Ian, but does not exist in their time now.

Brayden gathers enough information about Kayla, that once he has told them what he has learned, they know she was important to Ian. They will do whatever they can to help figure out what actually happened to Kayla for Ian.

***

It has been a month since Ian and the others made it to the school. Kenzie and Connor seem to have adjusted to their new life at school, which is also home for them now. Ian found out when he woke up, that he was asleep for three days. He did not know how much energy it took to use his gift, much less using it two times in a row. Once Ian is rested, he wakes up, eats, and then he is able to go to his own room. He has been in the school infirmary since his arrival. Ian is happy to find out that Brayden requested to be his roommate and wants to help him adjust to his new school. Brayden shows Ian were his classes are and where lunch is served. The school has a great library, which is one place Ian spends most of his free time.

In the month they have been at the school, there has been no word from Mason or Kayla. Ian uses his free time to work on contacting Kayla telepathically, but only Kenzie replies to his thoughts. Ian figures Kenzie is annoyed by all of his tries, but she never shows it. Thanks to Brayden's gift, he finds out more about Kayla, since Ian is the only one that even remembers her.

Now, since Kenzie knows about Kayla, she doesn't mind all the times Ian tries to contact Kayla telepathically. Kenzie can feel his pain every time he tries. She feels sorrow for him and hopes Kayla will answer him soon.

While Mason has made no attempts to break into the school or made any demands for Ian or Kenzie, they still cannot go too far from the school. They are never allowed to go anywhere alone outside the school grounds. There are a few places they can go, with a teacher or Jax, around Houston. One other place Ian loves to spend his free time, besides the library, is the Waterwall.

Ian spends any free time he has, when he is not in the library, at the Waterwall. The Waterwall was built in 1985, and it is 64 feet tall. The design of the Waterwall fountain is a semi-circle, like the shape of a horseshoe. The structure recycles 78,500 gallons of water every three hours and two minutes. It was also designed to give the illusion of a real waterfall. Ian goes there and sits for an hour, or two, just listening to the sound of the water rushing down the walls. It is relaxing to Ian.

Ian not only sits at the Waterwall for the sounds, but he is also hoping he can use the Waterwall to catch a glimpse Kayla. He does not know where she is, or if she is okay, but that doesn't stop him from trying.

It is on one of Ian's trips to the Waterwall, just as he heads out of the semi-circle fountain, when he hears a soft, faint voice in his head saying, *Don't let me be forgotten.* Ian knows that it is Kayla's voice. *I won't. I promise you,* Ian thinks back to the voice. Ian is not sure if he is just wanting to hear from her so bad that it is his mind playing tricks on him, or if it is really her speaking to him. But either way, he will never stop searching for answers. For now, he has to head back to the school.

Ian knows the more he learns about his gifts, the other's gifts, Mason, and even history itself, the more chances he has to find Kayla. He is determined to learn as much as he can about all of these things. School will be his whole world, at least until he can find his friend, Kayla, and restore her back in his history.

Chapter 15

Who is the Traitor?

"Well, they seemed to be ready for us. It's as if they had time to rest and strategize on their way here. One might think they knew we were not going to make a move on them until they made it here," Mason speaks loudly to his minions.

Everyone in the train station lobby begins looking around at one another, as if they don't understand the meaning of Mason's statement.

"What I'm trying to say is, it is like someone told them they would be safe until they made it here. They should not have felt safe at any time during their trip. They should have been on edge, looking over their shoulders for one of us to attack them. They should have been exhausted from not sleeping and always worrying, but they were none of those things. This suggests to me that there may be a traitor among us," Mason explains his earlier statement.

Mason's explanation leaves everyone looking straight at Kayla. They have all heard by now that Kayla is Ian's best friend and is now working with them, but they do not know any of the circumstances that have placed her there with them. Everyone is looking at Kayla except one person, and he is looking at Mason.

No one can tell he is not suspecting Kayla of being the traitor, as she is standing directly next to Mason. But he knows she is innocent, because it is *he* who is the traitor. He has been helping the others in a way that no one could ever imagine. See, he has the gift to take control over another person's body and mind at the same time. He does not have to be near them, nor does he have to have a bloodline connection to them. He has also been a part of Mason's group for several years, but his true intentions for becoming part of his team have never been revealed.

***

Before joining Mason's group, he was, and still remains, a part of a much higher power. His entire life has been nothing but training and learning history, which included learning about Jax, Ian, Kayla, and Mason. He has been learning about everyone in both groups, Mason's and Jax's. He has been sent to just observe the past, not to intervene with it.

His teachers think the best way to learn about history is to go back and to live it. In modern day terms, it is the same as reading a book for school and doing a book report on it for class, except they don't read when it is from. They don't read about it because they can, and do, access history in real time. To his culture, history is not really a past, but a mere moment of time in space. Since his world is separate from the history he studies, his teachers are unaware of anyone, other than them, being able to go back in to the past.

Once the rumors of Kayla becoming part of the group and yet being best friends with Ian started spreading, he does not understand what has happened. The history he has been sent to study mentions nothing of this event. This is not the history he has been taught and sent to watch. From that moment on, he felt something was wrong, or going to be wrong.

Knowing he is only there to observe the past and not to interfere with it, he feels he has no choice except to help out in any way he can to make the ending the exact same way as the one he has been sent to study.

***

Since he was accepted into Mason's group, over time he has been able to earn Mason's trust. He is not sure what that actually means in this world, but he knows it means something to this world's people. Even with Mason's trust, when Kayla comes into the picture, he keeps everyone at a distance from her. In this new history, he is not just watching it, but he is also a part of it. This not only excites him, but frightens him just the same. He knows he is out of his time, and world, but he also knows this is not the correct history for this world and time.

In an effort to get history back on the correct path, he knows he is going to have to break some rules of time travel. Knowing whatever actions he takes will not change his world, he knows he has to still be very careful about what he does in this time. Changing too much of this moment in this history can cause irreversible consequences for this history's future. If that were to happen, his teachers would know instantly and take him out of his studies. This would leave the moments he is supposed to be studying in turmoil.

He has to figure out something he can either do, or say to someone, that will be small, yet powerful enough to cause the exact time ripples needed to put things here back on the right track. He does not know exactly how much time he has, but he has to come up with something soon. This much he does know.

After taking a few days to recall all of the information he has obtained about this group of people he is studying, he remembers something that is never spoken of in the original version he previously learned. He believes it may be just enough to create a ripple effect to correct itself and still be small enough of a breach of protocols of time travel to not leave a devastating outcome if it does not work.

Now that he knows what he needs to do, he needs to come up with a plan on how to get this information to Kayla. She is the key to the success of his creative, yet mischievous, plan of action. He is going to have a hard time getting Kayla alone. Mason is either with her or has someone watching her at all times. He is still unsure what Kayla has to do with Mason's group, or why he has her under so much security, but he has to get to her one way or another.

Knowing his time is limited, he continues to get as close to Mason and Kayla as possible. He makes sure he attends every meeting Mason summons or any impromptu inspirational guidance he may start feeding his followers for the day. He is determined to find some pattern to their movements, so he will know where he can get Kayla alone just for a few minutes without drawing suspicion.

The more he watches their daily routines, the more he learns she is only alone at night in her bedroom with a guard at her door, and also when she goes to the restroom in the mornings to get ready for the day. He knows he has no shot at getting into either of those two places without being caught. He decides he only has one option to get the message to Kayla. He knows it's going to be a highly risky move, but he is left with no other choice.

***

"How dare you, coming into the bathroom as I am getting dressed!" Kayla is screaming at one of Mason's guards.

Kayla is now speaking loud and fast enough that the guard is unable to get a word in to try and explain his actions, before Mason comes rushing through the bathroom door.

"So, now you are having your guards watching me even in the bathroom?" Kayla questions Mason.

"Absolutely not! I would never violate your privacy. This is completely unacceptable and inexcusable. You two, take this man away from my sight and place him in the holding cell," Mason ends with an order to two other guards that arrived with him. "I am very sorry he came in here. Did he hurt you in any way?" Mason directs his question to Kayla.

"No, he did not hurt me, but I believe we have found your traitor," Kayla replies back.

"What makes you so sure that he is the traitor? What did he do?" Mason asks in return.

"Again, like I said before, he did nothing to hurt me. But the things he was saying to me makes him sound like a traitor."

"What did he say to you? I need you to be exact here."

"Well, to start with, when he first came into the room, he told me not to yell, because he was here to help me. Then he said he has been watching Ian and the others, making sure they are okay. Then he assured me that they made it safely to the school. After that is when he started to come towards me, saying he is going to get me out of here, and I had to go with him. That is when I started screaming at him," Kayla finishes with the details for Mason.

Mason's face has a stunned look on it. It is a look of shock and betrayal. "Is that everything he said to you?"

"Yes, that is all he said. He did not have much of a chance to say anything else, after I started screaming at him. I figured he was lying anyway, and that you had sent him in here to spy on me. But when you said you didn't order him to watch me in here, I began to think he was telling the truth. Wouldn't you say that sounds like a traitor?" Kayla snaps back at Mason.

"Yes, you are correct. That does sound like our traitor. I wonder how he has been able to communicate with them and not be detected. Since he did not reveal that information to you willingly, I will have to go down to the holding cell and get it from him myself. I have to find out if he is working alone or if others are involved. You understand, don't you?"

"If you say so. I really don't care about how you treat your crazy followers. I only care about how you and those nut-jobs treat me. You understand that, don't you?" Kayla replies back to Mason with some authority in her tone.

Mason gives Kayla a nod of understanding. Then he turns and walks out of the bathroom, shutting the door behind him.

Mason orders another follower to guard the door to the bathroom Kayla is in. "Make sure no one enters that room until I return. Do I make myself clear?" Mason commands the guard.

"Yes, sir," replies the newly appointed guard with pride in his voice for having such an important job.

Mason turns around again beginning his way down the long wide corridor. He is headed to the holding cell to speak to the guard who turned on them, the one Kayla says is the traitor. He is determined to end the distrust running among his group of followers. For right now, making sure the guard is working alone is his top priority.

The holding cell is in the basement of the building they occupy, so Mason stops at the elevator and presses the down call button. While waiting on the elevator to reach his floor, he begins to wonder to himself if Kayla is being truthful. *What does she have to gain by falsely accusing this guard of being a traitor? Does she know more than she is telling me?* Before he is able to finish his thoughts of Kayla making up this story, the doors to the elevator open, and he finds he has no more doubts about what Kayla has told him.

When the doors to the elevator open, they reveal the two guards he had instructed to take the traitor down to the cell are unconscious on the floor of the basement. It seems to Mason the traitor has been able to overpower these two guards and make an escape. This confirms he is a traitor, but this now leaves Mason with no way of finding out if he is working alone or not.

Chapter 16

Where do I Start?

Ian is going back and forth from writing off Kayla's voice, the one he hears in the semi-circle of the Waterwall, as his imagination overreacting, to wanting to believe it is her, to stopping dead in his tracks. *Kayla? Are you there?* Ian thinks out into space.

Yes. I'm here. Ian, there is something I need to tell you. Something extremely important. Are you somewhere you can sit and just listen for a few minutes? Kayla thinks her response back to Ian with a sense of urgency.

Are you kidding me? I'm the only person that even knows you exist. Of course, I have all the time you need! Ian's thinks back to Kayla with excitement.

Well, I don't have much time. That is why I need you to just listen to what I am about to tell you and not ask any questions, okay? There is so much I need to tell you, and questions will take up too much time to answer at this moment. Your questions will have to wait until I can contact you again. Promise? Kayla's thoughts are more of a plea to Ian rather than questions waiting to be answered by him.

Yes, I promise.

Okay. Many, many, many, years ago ...

***

Kayla only gets to spend a few minutes alone each day, since Mason decided to double cross Alexis. One of these times is being able to go to use the restroom alone. She used to make up any excuse she could to need to go to the restroom, until Mason figures out it is just to get away from him. Once he figures this out, he limits her time to the restroom to being able to use it to get ready in the morning, then she gets four restroom breaks during the day, then again before going to bed. With these limitations, she takes her private times very seriously.

The look on her face tells the guard, who has just come into the restroom during one of her private times unannounced, just how serious she takes these moments.

"Excuse me, but what do you think you are doing in here? I still have ten minutes left to get ready. How dare you just come in here and cut my time short. Has Mason put you up to this?" Kayla inquires of the guard.

"Kayla, I need you to listen to me for a moment. I am not the guard. I am currently in control of his mind and body. This is how I have been able to communicate with Ian and the others."

"Who are you? If this is true, then how do you know that I am even in this room, and the guard is on the outside of the door?" Kayla questions the guard's actual motivates.

"You have to trust me, Kayla. I am here with you, in this building. I am part of the group, but not in the way you, or Mason, would think. Let's say we may have some common interests. I'm not exactly sure why you are here, because you are not supposed to be. At least when and where I am from, this is not how history goes for you and Ian."

"What are you talking about? You sound just as crazy as the rest of Mason's clueless followers. Why should I believe anything you have to say?" Kayla asks the mystery guard with skepticism.

"What if I told you that I know, or knew, everything about you two? I have been assigned to study this part of your world's history, except something has been changed. You are never part of Mason's group from the history I've studied."

"Why do you keep saying history? History is the past, and we are not in the past, but the present. Are you part of Alexis's future?"

"Who is Alexis?"

"See, if you have been watching me and know all about me, then you would know who Alexis is. Now get out of here before I scream!" Kayla demands of the guard.

"You and Ian have known each other since you were small children. You two grew up together in the same walk up brownstone in Brooklyn, almost all your lives. You live one floor down from Ian. The two of you have been best friends since the first day you met in the lobby of that brownstone. That was also the day you and your family were moving in, so naturally, you were standing in front of the elevator doors when Ian and his mother walked in from shopping. That is when Ian informed you both about the elevator was not working. Actually he said, 'If you are waiting on the elevator, you will never be moved in. This elevator has never worked, so we have to take the stairs. They are right over here,' as he lead you both to the stairwell and walked with you until you reached your floor. You and your mother stepped out as they continued up to their floor. Now do you believe me?" he asks Kayla.

"There is no way anyone could know that. So I will have to say yes, I believe you. Because that *is* when we first met."

"Thank you, now may I continue? Neither of us have much time left alone to talk." He continues without an answer, "I am about to tell you something that no one knows. Something about how Ian's family and your family are related.

Your history says that Sebastian Helen, who is Ian's great, great, uncle, was the last known member of Peter Hele's bloodline to be in possession of the Time Keeper, before losing it after a fight with his best friend, Grayson Zimmerman. Peter Hele is the creator of the first watch, along with the Time Keeper, in case you are wondering. The stories told throughout your history say that Sebastian was an only child. This is not entirely true.

Sebastian's father actually had another child before him, except it was with another woman. Their relationship did not last long and was over before she found out she was with child. During those times, having a child out of wedlock was very shameful, not only to the woman, but to her entire family, current and future ones to come. Being that she was in a compromising position, she met another man very quickly, and had a short relationship before getting married. Before you ask, the reason she did not marry Sebastian's father is because he had met the woman he would marry, later in time, and had already moved to Danvers to be with her.

So, Sebastian had a half-sister he never knew about, who did have a wonderful happy family of her own. Therefore, the Hele family bloodline did not end with Sebastian. The bloodline is very much a long and healthy bloodline for many generations to come. The only difference is that his half-sister's family, until now, was not aware of their connection to the Time Keeper." He finishes his story.

"I don't understand what all of this has to do with me," Kayla interrupts.

"What I am trying to tell you is that a long time ago…"

***

...and that is why we have a connection through our thoughts, Kayla finishes thinking her explanation of what she learned from the guard.

WOW! That is a lot to take in at one time, Ian thinks back to Kayla.

I know. The only drawback from him taking over the guard's mind and body was that once he lost his connection with the guard, the guard knew our entire conversation. So in order for me to try and keep it from Mason, I started to scream at the guard. I acted like the guard walked in on me in the middle of getting dressed, so I started screaming at him and kept talking loud enough for him not to be able to get a word out of his mouth, all the way up until Mason showed up and had the guard taken away just now, down to some holding cell. Kayla's thoughts are beginning to take a toll on her mind, her thoughts sound like a strain on her.

Now I am worried because I came up with a story, making the guard out to be a traitor in Mason's group. Now Mason is on his way down to the holding cell to talk to the guard, alone, to question him to see if he is working with anyone else. Of course he is not working with anyone else, because he is not the traitor, but he knows who is and what he told me. When Mason gets down to the cell and speaks to the guard, he will find out I am lying.

Ian, I have to go! I think something is wrong, because Mason is already on his way back. I can hear him yelling at the guards in the hallway. I can't make out what he is saying, but he doesn't sound happy.

He's at the door now. I'm sorry, Ian. I have to go. Kayla finishes her thoughts to Ian, before breaking off the connection with him.

Kayla! Kayla? Are you still there? Are you okay? Ian tries to get Kayla to think back to him, but his tries fall flat.

As Ian is about to start yelling for Kayla out loud with his actual voice, one of the teachers from his school appears from around the corner entry of the semi-circle of the Waterwall.

"Jax sent me to get you. He says it's time for your studies today," the teacher instructs Ian.

"Yes, let's head back to the school, I have to speak to Jax as soon as possible," Ian demands of the teacher.

As Ian and his teacher make their way back to the school to meet with Jax, Ian is thinking of ways to prove what Kayla told him is true. Even though Jax and his friends are coming around to believing him more about Kayla, he stills thinks it's too early for them to start believing stories from her. He knows he is going to need something concrete to show them before they believe this story.

Saving History – School Bound

Ian is so caught up in his own thoughts he does not even notice when they arrive at the school. Once he recognizes where he is, he opens the back door of the car service they used to get from the Waterwall to the school, gets out as fast as he can and runs in through the front doors of the school. Upon entering the building, Ian begins his way to the library. He decided, on the way from the Waterwall, that the library will be a great place for him to start to look for any trace of Sebastian's half-sister.

Ian takes the elevator to the twelfth floor, which is the first floor of the library. The library itself take up three floors of the building. The school library is almost as impressive as the New York Library, with the exception of this library containing information pertaining to everything that is left out of the normal human world. The books here are filled with the true stories of magic, witchcraft, and all things supernatural, which the regular humans claim as folklore and fairytales.

Remembering the entire story Kayla repeated to him from the guard about Sebastian's half-sister, Ian makes his way over to a computer sitting on the desk in the center of the room. With only a few quick keystrokes, Ian is able to locate the section of the library where the history of Sebastian and his father are kept. Ian figures that is the best place to start if he wants to learn more about the life Sebastian's father had before having him. Now that Ian has his starting point, all he has to do is make his way to his new location in the library and get to work.

After a brisk walk through the maze of books, he reaches Sebastian's family's section. He finds the first book of their family history, finds the nearest seat, and begins to journey back in history to learn as much as he can to find the proof he needs to convince the others of the story. Before long, Ian finds out that there is nothing in their history books about Sebastian's father having had a child before Sebastian. It was just as Kayla said, no one knew except the mother. Ian is going to go nowhere if he pursues this course of investigating. Time to change things up and think of something else.

Knowing he needs to change his way of searching for this half-sister, Ian tries to think back to see if Kayla mentioned the other woman's name, or even the sisters' name, but comes up with nothing. *Why did she leave out the woman's name, or Sebastian's half-sister's name, throughout the entire story?* Ian wonders to himself.

"Well, it's time I face Jax and tell him what I know, or better yet, what Kayla has told me. Maybe he will be able to shed some light on this matter," Ian thinks out loud, as he closes the book of his family history and places it back on the bookshelf.

***

How am I going to be able to convince Jax, and the others, what Kayla has told me is true? Since it was never spoken of in history or written about, which I double checked, then there is no way to prove the story she was told is true. This is going to be a battle, Ian thinks to himself while on his way to the find Jax.

Ian makes his way over to the elevators by navigating through the walls of books. Now that he is ready to tell Jax what he knows, he just needs to find him. He was not informed about where Jax wanted to meet with him when he was picked up at the Waterwall by the teacher, so he decides to try something while waiting on the elevator to arrive.

Hey, Kenzie? Are you with Jax right now?

Ian? Where have you been? Everyone has been looking for you, is Kenzie's reply to Ian's thoughts.

Why? What is so important to have everyone looking for me? Has something happened?

I'm not sure exactly, but Jax seems to think something is going on.

That must be why he sent the teacher to pick me up from the Waterwall. Where is Jax now?

He and the others are in the Sky Lounge, on the roof. It's in the same location of the pool you brought us through, from the Houston Train Station fountain.

Thank you, Kenzie. I'll head that way now. Are you going up there as well?

Yes. I just came down to check on Connor. He's fine, so I'll meet you there. Kenzie finishes their telepathic conversation.

As their conversation ends, the elevator doors open. Ian steps inside and presses the button for the top floor. The doors close and the elevator, and Ian, make their way up until they reach their destination, the roof. Ian steps out of the elevator and takes a left for a few steps, then another left towards the Sky Lounge door. To Ian's surprise, when he opens the door, Jax and Brayden are sitting at a table with a woman. She is not anyone that Ian has ever met before.

Ian makes his way over to their table, and upon reaching them, Jax introduces Ian to Maria, the head of the Believers. They exchange pleasantries and decide to wait on Kenzie before they begin with the meeting. While they wait, Ian's mind takes over with his own thoughts.

Why is the head of the Believers, Maria, here and where do I even begin with what Kayla has told me? Well, I guess...... the beginning is a good place to start.

Epilogue: Council's Invitations Sent

With the invitations sent out to the leaders of the three groups they narrowed down to their choices to help them go back in time, the council members begin to prep the meeting hall. They are preparing for the Special Council Meeting with anticipation for all three group leaders, even before knowing who will accept their invitation.

***

Fisher is the leader of the Aquarians. They reside in the depths of the unexplored areas of the oceans. As the oceans cover over seventy percent of the earth, with only twenty percent of its entirety actually being explored and mapped, they are able to flourish as a species with no known enemies.

The Aquarians are larger than the entire population of the land people on the planet, yet only the Council knows of their existence. So when Fisher receives an invitation from the Council, he knows it must be of some importance. He does not believe the Council would risk revealing their existence to anyone else, unless they have no other options.

Fisher takes the invitation, opens it, and reads its contents. It begins with...

***

Emma is not actually the leader of the Fairley's. Since they are such a free spirited people, they have no leaders. Emma volunteers to receive the invitation from the Council on behalf of the Fairley people. In volunteering to accept the invitation, she has also accepted any and all responsibilities the invitation may ask of her people. To Emma, this is a very high honor.

Emma, being a free spirit, is very excited for the responsibility she has accepted, since the Fairley people are everywhere above water. They live in the forests, parks, cities, small towns, the deserts, and even the caves of the mountains. Having the full support and trust of all the Fairley behind her, even though she is only twelve years old, is a sign of respect.

Even though Fairley's are known among the many people of the world, this is the first time they have ever received a special invitation from the Council. With this being a first for their people, Emma understands this must be an urgent matter.

Emma takes the invitation, opens it, and reads its contents. It begins with ...

***

For over 400 years, Travis has watched over the Windairian people. His people are what humans classify as anyone with any type of magical power, but that is not exactly true of the Windairians. Humans tend to put things that they don't understand, or are afraid of, into categories and classifications, so naturally they are both when it comes to Magic. The Windairians can live among the humans, if they choose, but they are a people of the sky. They travel by wind and air from place to place.

Travis has always watched his people from the clouds, or from the highest mountain peaks, or if he has to, down on the actual ground. That is usually on a cloudless day, and he is needed to be in a certain area to keep an eye on a situation involving his people. Otherwise, he uses the air and wind to pass over the world to watch them from afar and without notice.

The Windairians have been called upon by the Council before, so when Travis receives their invitation, before even reading it, he has mentally already accepted whatever is asked of him and his people. The Council has always watched out for the Windairians, and his people, in return, vowed to always help The Council when called.

Travis takes the invitation, opens it, and reads its contents. It begins with …

***

Word travels fast throughout the world, through every group the Council watches, even those who do not approve of the Council's oversight, but tolerate it.

"The Fairley's and the Windairians have each received an invitation from the Council, yet there is no word on who the third people are,"

Preston tells his younger brother, Payton. "It is said that all three invitations have reached who they were sent to, so it's no mistake that the Council did not send one to us."

"Do you actually expect them to ask for our help after the last time?" Payton replies to Preston with laughter.

"That is not the point here, Brother. *We* are one of the most powerful people they know. What can they need, or want, that they do not want us to know about?" Preston puts Payton's questions to a halt with his authoritative tone.

Preston and Payton are brothers, but Preston is the first born, making him the King of the Ember people, and leaving Payton the Prince. King Preston and Prince Payton's people live in the Under Earth, the hottest crust layers of Earth. When they get upset, the people of Earth see a rise in volcanic activity and wildfires, which is exactly what happened the last time the Council requested their help.

"What are you planning to do?" Prince Payton asks the King.

"Let's send them one of our own invitations to remind them that we are here and just how powerful we are. I'm sure that we can persuade them to see the error of their ways and send a fourth invitation to us before the end of the day," the King finishes with excitement.

"Now, I need you to go and tell the others …"

***

"We knew the King of the Embers would find out about the invitations. Did we really expect him not to show some anger in not receiving one? We have no choice. We must send him one now, and quickly, or the big island of Hawaii, Kona, will never survive these volcanic eruptions. The Island of Kona is our largest and oldest museum of the world's past. We must protect it at all cost. So, if it means inviting those Brothers to this meeting, then so be it. Send the invitation to the King of the Embers," orders the head of the Council. "What could go wrong?"

Acknowledgements

I would like to thank my Grandmother, Billie Young and my uncle Marty Young of Enloe, TX, for always being there for me when I needed them. Also, to my mom and dad, Donna and John Capell, you both have always helped me when I needed it and also taught me how to make it on my own. From the depths of my heart, thank you both for that. Then again, to my brother Pete, for the amazing paintings which are the very colorful parts of the cover arts you see on both "Time Keeper" and "School Bound".

Next, I would like to thank my editor, Patricia, of Carpenter Editing Services, LLC. She has been a second mother to me for many years and with her editing skills, advice, and opinions on "Time Keeper" and now "School Bound" this work of art would not be what it is today. She brings such joy in my writing with her suggestions and honest critiques. Not to mention, her patience with me has been amazing. With my reading disability, she has been able to teach me more about proper English and being able to become a better writer. Along with my Editor, I need to thank my Beta Reader, Jordan Eagles, whose feedback was amazing and helped create this final product.

I could not leave out a thank you to the rest of my family for allowing me to use their names as the majority of my characters. I chose my family for character names because my family members are all characters in their own way. They are in no way like their characters in this book, but they are all very special and unique people in their own right. "Jax" is one of my heroes and is also one of the reasons for this book series. My nephew Jaxon is an amazing special child, with two loving parents, my little brother John Dock and my sister-in-law Jessica. They also raised a lovely daughter, Kenzie; who made her appearance in this book, along with my little sister Ashley's son, Brayden. Thank you to Kayla and Alexis for opening book one.

Now I have to thank my Aunt and Uncle, Delores and Jerry Green, who are not villains in real life, but I think are from a different time. Also from my side of the family I introduced my cousins Travis, Fisher, Preston and Payten, Jerry and Delores' grandchildren.

Also, it is awesome to have introduced Connor and Emma, two of Patricia's grandchildren. Connor's opinions have made a big difference in the outcome in this installment.

I would also like to give a quick thank you to the places that allowed me to sit and write in their establishments when I needed that creative energy. A few of those places are Overtime Grill and Bar (off Lakeshore Pkwy in Birmingham, AL), Rose who is also a character introduced in this installment works at Overtime, Dunkin Donuts (off HWY 119 in Pelham, AL) and 700 Riverchase (in Hoover, AL), Railroad Park (Birmingham, AL). Without these places listed I would have been lost, because as someone with ASD, social settings are not easy for me, and I never felt out of place or any pressure at these creative energy spots. These places made me feel at home every time.

Last, but not least, Maria Dore. For without her reading my short story, "Time Lost", and then telling me "The End? I don't think so. I want more!" This series would not exist today. She herself is a character, and made it into the series.

Thank you Maria for always pushing me in work and out of work.

Robert Starnes

Continue along with Ian, as he continues to find a way to save his best friend, Kayla, in *Search Begins*.

An Exciting and Adventurous way to view History

Book Three of the

Saving History Series

Search

Begins

Robert Starnes

Robert Starnes

Prologue: Council's Invitations Answered

The Council knew this special meeting they have called would have a few setbacks and possible conflicts. This thought was a possibility before they were forced to invite the Royal Brothers of the Embers. Before they were coerced by the Royal Brothers, Preston and Payton, their biggest concern was how to make sure the largest, unknown species, the Aquarians, remained secret from all other groups, tribes, and humans alike. The Aquarians have lived in the oceans for so long, undetected, as humans have only been able to actually research twenty percent of the oceans, which the oceans make up seventy percent of the Earth. They know they can trust the Fairley's and Windairians, but the unpredictability of the Embers made them question if any of the others would show, now that the Brothers were formally invited.

The Council has already made preparations for a meeting of five, still hoping that the original three groups will attend the meeting. The Council has received no replies regarding anyone refusing to attend the meeting, which they take as a good sign.

Now the day has arrived, and they will find out if the invitation to the Embers was a mistake. They do not have to wait long before the first of their invited guests arrive out in front of the meeting hall. The hall has a circular driveway with a large Angelic water fountain in the center of it. The first to arrive is Emma, the representative of the Fairley Folk, accompanied by her friend Rose. Upon arrival, the two of them are greeted by the Council, escorted inside the meeting hall, and taken to their seats at the table.

Next to arrive is Travis, the leader of the Windairians, traveling alone. Travis is greeted by the Council and ushered inside the meeting hall in the same manner as Emma and Rose were. Travis is lead to a seat next to Emma, and as he is taking his seat, the Royal Brothers of the Embers, Preston and Payton, make their grand entrance into the meeting hall. They were not greeted upon arrival and are unescorted to their seats. Needing no introductions to the others, they make their way to the open seats on the opposite side of the table from the Fairley's and Windairian.

The Council leaves the groups inside and heads back outside for two reasons. One is to simply get away from King Preston, and the second is to make sure Fisher, the Aquarian leader, has a proper welcome, if he comes. The Council knows the importance of keeping the Aquarian people unknown to the world, and understands if Fisher has changed his mind, and now declines their invitation due to Preston and Payton's invitation. The Council waits for thirty minutes and assumes Fisher has changed his mind, to protect his people. They then turn and walk back inside the council meeting hall.

As the Council enters through the doors of the hall, commotion between the three groups left alone inside the room is the only thing to be heard. The Council can see his absence was a mistake, walking over to the table and taking his position as the Council Leader. Before he can take control over the unruly groups, they have all come to an eerie quiet. They are no longer arguing and yelling amongst themselves, but merely staring at the tall, green, quiet man walking into the room. It is Fisher, the Aquarian leader.

Here we go, the Council leader thinks to himself, walking over greeting Fisher, then walking him over to his place at the table. Fisher takes his seat, while the others keep their stance and stare, until the Council draws all of their attention to his direction. He asks them all to take their seats and listen to why he has summoned them all here today. To his surprise, they all obey his command, leaving the floor open for the Council to speak.

And so, the Council begins...

Chapter 1

Who Trusts Whom?

Once Ian had everyone in the Sky Lounge of the school, he repeated the story Kayla had told him about Sebastian having a half-sister. He also told them about how he was unable to find any information about this previous child by Sebastian's father. As he finishes, he receives the exact reaction he expected from them, blank faces staring back at him.

"Okay, don't everyone speak at the same time," Ian tries to joke with the group.

"How sure are you that this story is true?" Jax asks Ian.

"One hundred percent true. Kayla has no reason to lie to me. She wants to be back in our timeline just as much as I want her back," Ian stands his ground on the validity of the story he was told by Kayla.

"Well, this is news to me. Who is Kayla and what does she have to do with any of this?" Maria is asking no one in particular.

"So, Maria, haven't you been the person Jax always runs to for information from the Council?" Ian directs his question.

"I would not put it exactly that way, but yes, Jax does receive important updates from me, in regards to anything of concern to the Believers," Maria answers Ian's question.

"And who do you get your information from? If you don't mind me asking?" Ian replies.

"Where is all of this coming from, Ian? Maria has given us some very good and accurate information on matters at hand during our entire trip. Why are you questioning her or the information she has given me during our mission to get here?" Jax is now stepping in before Maria can even answer Ian's question.

"Because, either the information she has been given was not fully accurate, or she has been leaving out information from you," Ian explains to Jax.

"How do you figure," Maria is back to asking the questions.

"Well, to be honest, how is it that no one in the Council knew about Sebastian's half-sister?

And how is it that none of you were even aware of Kayla, Kenzie, and Connor, considering Kenzie has some very powerful abilities?" Ian is demanding answers from Maria.

"What exactly has Jax told you about the Council, and what do you think we do?" Maria asks back to Ian.

"From what I understand, the original Council members each gave up one of their own children to create the Believers. This was done because of Sebastian and his continued use of the Time Keeper. The Believers have been around ever since to help make sure that the Time Keeper remains in possession of the next in line of the Hele bloodline. Now, they were never able to directly intervene by showing the next in line where the Time Keeper was, once it was lost, but they could, however, spread rumors to lead them to it. As far as the Council goes, I am afraid Jax has not told me very much more about it, but I suspect that if the original Council members could give up their own children to create the Believers, then they must have some major power, or control, over others," Ian gives Maria a short, but accurate summary.

"I'm impressed. Jax has given you a very good history lesson on the Believers and how they were created. But it sounds like you know nothing else of the Council. Now that we have cleared that up, would you like to explain why you think we gave Jax incorrect information on purpose?" Maria asks Ian for clarification.

"I don't have to know what you do, exactly, to know that information you gave is incorrect. As powerful as I suspect you are, if you are giving information to Jax, then you were given the information, or you know where to look to find out the answers. So, again I will ask you, how is it that you do not know about Sebastian's half-sister, Kayla, Kenzie, or Connor? I don't mean to be so blunt, but we don't have time to compare notes on what I know about the Believers and what I don't. We need to know about that half-sister," Ian demands.

***

"Guards!" Once the elevator made it back to his floor, Mason yells down the hallway, as he finds the other two guards laid out cold on the elevator floor and the traitor missing. "Guards! What happened here? Where is the Traitor?"

Kayla is still in the bathroom, having just broken off her connection with Ian. She has no idea what's happening outside in the hallway, but she is scared. Scared that Mason has found out the truth. The truth that she has lied to him that there is someone else who is the real traitor.

She is pacing the bathroom floor when the knock on the door comes. "Kayla? It's me, Mason. Open the door please. We have a situation," Mason is not asking Kayla, and she knows it.

Kayla walks over to the bathroom door, half scared to open it, but she knows she has no choice. If she does not open the door, he will get in one way or another. She decides it's best to face this willingly.

Kayla grabs the bathroom door knob and gives it a slow turn. She did not have to unlock the door, because she never locked it when the guard, whose body was used to tell her the story about Sebastian's half-sister, was taken away and Mason left her in here to go interrogate him alone.

Kayla takes a deep breath and opens the door. *I guess this is it for me!*

As the door opens, Mason is standing there, looking at Kayla. Neither of them speaks for a few seconds. Mason is the first to break the awkward silence.

"Are you alone?"

"Yes, why wouldn't I be? You just left me here, and it was just us two in here. What's going on?"

"The traitor has somehow escaped. As I made it to the elevator to go down to speak to him, the elevator came up and the doors opened, and the guards that were sent to escort him to his cell were out cold on the elevator floor. The traitor is gone," Mason explains the events that happened out in the hallway.

How is this possible? How can the guard just escape? Kayla wonders to herself before asking Mason. "How did this happen? What kind of guards do you have working for you? You have had them watching my every minute, but I feel if I were in danger, they could not help me. They obviously can't even protect themselves. What are you going to do now?" Kayla asks Mason, with a hit of sarcasm in her tone.

Mason feels her sarcasm and threatens her back, "Do not worry about my guards. They are fine and *will* protect you, if I ask them to. Or they will just report to me your every movement, if I ask them to do that. I think you should choose your next words very carefully because what you say next will determine what orders I will give the guards that pertain to you and your safety." Kayla fully understands exactly what Mason means, so instead of saying anything, at the moment, she gives him a quick nod.

"Now as far as the traitor goes, we will deal with him once we catch him. There is no way he has been able to leave this place. So, he is here, somewhere, and he will be found. I will tell you this, his actions do, however, support your theory of him being the traitor. I'm sorry I doubted your assumption about him," Mason finishes.

"I'm sorry as well. I'm sorry that one of your trusted guards is the traitor. I know you don't trust people easily, so being betrayed by him must hurt you pretty badly," Kayla apologies back to Mason.

"Thank you, but I have a feeling you have something else you are wanting to say."

"I don't want to upset you, or overstep my place, but this is exactly what you did to Alexis. You promised her you would protect me, but instead you turned around and betrayed her and keep me as a prisoner. Now you know how she would have felt if she knew this is what you would have done to her," Kayla tells Mason.

"You made your point very clear, Kayla. But you forget, Alexis is not here, and she abandoned you with me. If she knew anything about me, then she would have known she could not trust me. That means that all the things she told me about her being from the future were a lie. Someone from the future would have already known I was going to betray them, so why would she leave you with me?" Mason tries to contradict Alexis's mission of changing the future. He also wants to make sure Kayla remembers just how she ended up with him.

"Have you ever stopped to think that this is part of her plan in order for the future to change? Maybe she knew of your betrayal, maybe she didn't. I can tell you one thing: time will tell if she knew or not. I have a feeling inside that Alexis knows what she is doing and things will work out the way she plans them to, with you anyway," Kayla snaps back in defense of Alexis.

"For your sake, I hope you are right, but I doubt anything she said is true," Mason ends their conversation, while turning around to lead them out of the bathroom and into the hallway to start the manhunt for the traitor.

***

"So, what you are saying is that you have, or had, a best friend named Kayla, who somehow was erased from time, yet you are the only person who can not only remember her, but also can speak to her? And you want to question the information I have given Jax?" Maria speaks harshly to Ian.

Ian knows now that telling Maria about Kayla is a mistake. Luckily for him, he has a quick fix for this. Ian takes a moment to store this memory in the Time Keeper. This is the first time he has used it to store a memory of his own in it, so he is excited to say the least. He will not access this memory now, but will let it play out to see the outcome, before going in and changing it yet.

"Yes, that is correct. You would think that the Council would have noticed a major change in time, wouldn't you? I don't care if you believe me or not, I know that Sebastian has a half-sister, and I know Kayla is real. If you won't help me look for answers, or a way to get Kayla back, then I will continue looking on my own," Ian states to Maria, as he is turning around and walking out of the Sky Lounge.

Don't worry Kayla, I will never give up on getting you back, Ian thinks telepathically into space, hoping Kayla can hear him.

The elevator doors open, Ian steps inside and presses the button for the library floor to continue his search for answers.

About the Author

Robert Starnes is not only the author of *The Multifamily Housing Guide Series: Leasing 101 - Garden Style*, and *The Saving History Series: Time Keeper* and *School Bound*, but he is also the publisher. He created Starnes Books LLC so he could have full control over his work and to be able to help other self-publish authors with free advice on what they can do to save money and not be taken for their hard work.

After being diagnosed with Asperger's Syndrome, which it is now part of a broader category called ASD (Autism Spectrum Disorder), at the age of 43, things started to click with him. After being able to identify and manage the parts of ASD he had, he was able to hone in on his creative writing. At a young age he did not like to read, because he had difficulty with the words on the pages in front of him. He knew the words and understood them, but his brain would comprehend them faster than his voice could speak them. This would cause him to either leave out words, or cause him to read very slowly so he could have his eyes go back over the words again, two to three times, before his voice caught up with his brain. This embarrassment would stop him from reading for many years.

As an adult learning to face his fears, he began to read John Grisham novels. He loves the law and movies, so it was perfect for him to read the "The Last Juror" before watching the movie. After reading such a great novel then watching the movie, he quickly learned he enjoyed comparing the differences between the novels and the movies. That was all it took for him to begin to enjoy reading for the first time. For many years he would only read novels that were going to become movies, because that was what he enjoyed about reading. After many years, he read another novel that became a movie, but they never completed the movie series. The novel was so good that he completed the book series, which in turn gave him a new enjoyment for reading without the novels becoming movies.

With this in Robert's mind, he has written his series for anyone that may be going through the same things he went through as a child, or adult, with reading, and is trying to find a way for them to connect with the world of reading. He believes that you can read and write a perfectly great action packed novel that does not have to be 800 pages thick to be accomplished. He believes giving someone the opportunity and a way to enter the world of reading, then that's the accomplishment. No one should be afraid to read or write in their own style for others to be able to want to read. His mind does not work the same as a traditional writer's does and retains things much more than another person's may, so you will not find very much repeating, or recapping, in his series. You will find action, adventure, and history from the very first chapter to the very end.

To Robert, everyone is different and unique, and should be celebrated every day for being just who they are. He finds that when life may get you down, you can always get away in your own imagination with the help of a good book.

He was born in Texas, but now does most of his writing in Alabama. To learn more about him and his books, visit starnesbooksllc.com, or follow @Starnes_Books on twitter, and find @starnesbooksllc on Instagram.

Robert Starnes

Books by Robert Starnes

Saving History Series:

Time Keeper – Starnes Books LLC (2018)
School Bound – Starnes Books LLC (2019)

The Multifamily Housing Guide Series

Leasing 101: Garden Style – Starnes Books, LLC (2018)

The Multifamily Housing Guide – *Leasing 101 Garden Style Edition* – Lulu's publishing (2016 retired print)

Robert Starnes

CPSIA information can be obtained
at www.ICGtesting.com
Printed in the USA
FFHW020051210719
53758371-59459FF